KT-160-957

THE BEST SLEEPOVER IN THE WORLD

JACQUELINE WILSON

Illustrated by *Rachael Dean*

PUFFIN

PUFFIN BOOKS

UK | USA | Canada | Ireland | Australia
India | New Zealand | South Africa

Puffin Books is part of the Penguin Random House group of companies
whose addresses can be found at global.penguinrandomhouse.com.

www.penguin.co.uk
www.puffin.co.uk
www.ladybird.co.uk

Neath Port Talbot Libraries	
2400041587	
PETERS	19-Oct-2023
	14.99
NPTSKE	

MAKATON is a trade mark belonging to The Makaton Charity.

All third-party website links are included for information purposes only and the author and
publisher accept no responsibility for, and do not control, approve or endorse, any information
or material contained on such third-party websites or social media platforms.

Text design by Janene Spencer
Set in Baskerville MT Pro 14.5/24pt

Printed in Great Britain by Clays Ltd, Elcograf S.p.A.

The authorized representative in the EEA is Penguin Random House Ireland,
Morrison Chambers, 32 Nassau Street, Dublin D02 YH68

A CIP catalogue record for this book is available from the British Library

HARDBACK ISBN: 978–0–241–56722–7

INTERNATIONAL PAPERBACK ISBN: 978–0–241–56723–4

All correspondence to:
Puffin Books
Penguin Random House Children's
One Embassy Gardens
8 Viaduct Gardens
London SW11 7BW

MIX
Paper from
responsible sources
FSC® C018179

Penguin Random House is committed to a
sustainable future for our business, our readers
and our planet. This book is made from Forest
Stewardship Council® certified paper.

For Lucinda and her mum, Nikki

Chapter One

It's a bit rubbish when you move and have to go to a new school. Everyone else has had years to make friends. You're just the new girl who hasn't *got* any friends. But on my very first day Emily was so kind.

She saw me hovering at the edge of the classroom, came up to me and asked my name. I mumbled 'Daisy' and she said she liked flower names. Then she said, 'I think your plaits look great. I'm trying to

grow my hair but it's taking ages.'

So I said, 'I think your bunches look really cute,' and then we smiled at each other.

She lent me her spare pen, showed me where the toilets were at playtime and said I could sit on her table at lunchtime because there was an empty seat.

Three other girls sat with Emily: Amy, Bella and Chloe. Amy had a special way of saying hello to me, which involved a lot of clapping hands and high-fiving. I got the hang of it the second time, and she said I was a quick learner.

Bella gave me a square of chocolate from her packed lunch. We're not supposed to bring *any* chocolate to school, and the Dinner Lady Police confiscate it if they spot it, but Bella's brilliant at hiding it in her pocket.

'*Umm!* I'm telling on both of you,' said Chloe.

She waved her hand in the air to attract the attention of the frowniest dinner lady, who was busy mopping up a puddle on the floor because two boys had been mucking about with their glasses of water. 'Miss! Miss, can you come over here, please?' Chloe called.

My heart started thumping underneath my new uniform. I'd only been at this school half a day and already I was in trouble.

The dinner lady came stomping over, her lips pressed together so tightly her mouth disappeared. I thought I was definitely in for it – *and* poor Bella. But Chloe simply looked up at the dinner lady, opening her eyes wide and giving her a sweet smile.

'Sorry to trouble you, miss, but the new girl wants a drink of water though she's too shy to ask,' said Chloe, quick as a flash.

The dinner lady tutted. 'You just fetch yourself a glass from that table on the side, silly,' she said, and went back to mopping.

Chloe giggled. 'Your faces, you two!' she said. 'I was only joking. Better give me the rest of your chocolate though, Bell, or I *might* tell.'

Bella stuck her tongue out at her, not looking too bothered – but she gave her the chocolate anyway. Emily looked upset. She didn't say anything, but she felt for my hand under the table and gave it a little squeeze.

'Sorry about that. Chloe likes to play jokes,' she muttered to me when we went out into the playground. 'She doesn't really mean to be horrid.'

Yes she did. Chloe was clearly The Boss. And, worst of all, Emily was clearly her best friend.

We were this awkward fivesome for a while,

Amy and Bella and Emily and Chloe and me. It was sheer bliss when Chloe was off school for a week with flu. It was probably just a sniffle. Chloe's parents are always fussing over her – especially her dad.

I was free to be proper friends with Emily. We liked doing exactly the same things. We loved reading and making up our own stories and colouring. We told each other our secrets. Emily said she was really fed up with her baby brother, Ben, because he yelled all the time, though she supposed he couldn't help it because he was only little. I almost told her about my sister, Lily, who can't walk or talk. She used to yell a lot too, though not so much now she's at her new school. I suppose *she* can't help it when she gets upset either. But I didn't want to talk about Lily. Not yet. What if Emily was funny about it?

Emily said she didn't want to be friends with Chloe any more because she could be so mean.

'Then why don't you break friends with her and be *my* best friend?' I asked.

I knew why. She was a bit scared of Chloe. Actually, so was I. But we didn't have to be scared of her ANY MORE!

We all had birthdays during the summer term. Amy had a sleepover with a huge chocolate birthday cake, and we danced and painted our nails, and I thought it was the best sleepover party ever.

Then Bella had a birthday sleepover and she had a fantastic swimming-pool cake, and we went swimming at the leisure centre, then we all crammed into a big double bed and got the giggles. I thought *that* was the best sleepover party ever.

Then Emily had a birthday sleepover and had

a teddy-bear birthday cake, and we played football. I got to share Emily's bed and I knew *that* simply had to be the best sleepover party ever.

Then Chloe had a sleepover party and deliberately didn't invite me. Emily said she didn't want to go to Chloe's sleepover if I couldn't come. Amy and Bella said they wouldn't attend Chloe's sleepover party either. So then Chloe invited me too, and I went to her sleepover in her big, posh house.

We made our own pizzas but Chloe spoiled mine. She had an amazing birthday cake with three

layers, but I didn't dare eat a single mouthful because I thought Chloe might have done something to my slice. I couldn't share a bed with Emily. I didn't share a bed with anyone. I was stuck in an old sleeping bag by myself. That was definitely the WORST sleepover ever.

I had a birthday cake in the shape of a daisy for *my* sleepover. Emily met Lily for the first time. I was worried but Emily was lovely to her. Lily liked her too – and Amy and Bella. But then Lily got frightened and had to be put to bed before Chloe arrived.

We watched a movie Chloe had given me – but it was SCARY – and then Chloe laughed at us for being scared. It looked like my own sleepover was turning into the worst sleepover in the world. But Dad put up a tent in the garden and we slept out

there, and it was FUN. Then Chloe woke up and wanted to go to the loo.

I had to take her indoors to show her where it was. Lily heard and wailed like a ghost – and Chloe was so frightened she cried and WET HERSELF! She had to be taken home even though it was the middle of the night. Emily, Amy, Bella, Lily and I played together in the morning, and it became the BEST sleepover in the world.

And the most amazing thing happened. Chloe broke friends with all of us because she was so embarrassed that we all knew she wet herself. She's got another little gang of girls now. Emily and I are

best friends for ever and we go around with Amy and Bella. We steer clear of Chloe and she keeps well away from us.

It was so brilliant – but then . . .

Chapter Two

Chloe burst into our classroom before school started, her cheeks pink, her blonde hair carefully curled, her little gold stud earrings glinting, her high-heeled shoes clicking (definitely *not* school uniform policy). She did a little dance in her amazing shoes, ending with a flourish.

'Ta dah!' she said, spreading her arms wide.

Her new girly gang clapped her in a sickening

way. Not just the girls. Sam and Richard actually cheered. They vie with each other to be Chloe's boyfriend. Mum says we're far too young to have boyfriends in junior school. Tell that to Chloe! She tosses her hair and stands with her hand on her hip, as if she's posing for a photograph. Emily and I roll our eyes and tut but Sam and Richard think she's fabulous. Pathetic!

'Hey, listen up, you guys,' said Chloe. Apparently it's the way Mattie Rayburn talks. She's a famous TikTok star who does that Prance Dance. I haven't actually seen her because Mum won't let me have my own mobile yet and she doesn't have TikTok on her phone.

Amy's big sisters have taught her to do the Prance Dance and she's shown us. It's very complicated. Emily and I can't do it properly yet. Chloe laughs her head off at us and calls us losers. Who cares? At least we don't wet ourselves.

No one was 'listening up' except the Girl Gang and Sam and Richard. Chloe clapped her hands imperiously.

'*Listen*, I said. You'll never ever guess what,' she announced, tossing her curls.

My hair goes a bit like that when I undo my

plaits, but it's not quite as fluffy. It's very annoying having to admit it, but Chloe has lovely hair.

'What, Chloe?' the Girl Gang begged in a chorus.

'Tell us, Chloe,' said Sam.

Richard simply gazed at her adoringly. I'm not sure he wants to be her actual boyfriend. I think he wants to *be* her.

'Well!' said Chloe. 'I'm only going to have the best sleepover party in the entire world.'

We were listening properly now. Emily wrinkled her nose.

'How come she's having a sleepover?' she murmured. 'She's already had her birthday.'

I remembered my awful spoiled pizza and shuddered. 'She's only showing off to get everyone's attention,' I whispered. 'I bet she's bluffing.'

Chloe's ears were sharp even though they were hidden under all that hair.

'I am *so* having another sleepover,' she said. 'There's no law that says sleepover parties have to be about birthdays. I'm having *my* sleepover just because.'

'Because what?' said Amy.

'She'd better watch out. Remember what happened at Daisy's sleepover!' said Bella.

We all giggled, but Emily frowned at us.

'Don't be mean,' she whispered. 'Don't tell on her. It would be awful if the whole class laughed about her.'

She doesn't like Chloe any more. She's glad she's not friends with her now. It's just that she's kind. I try to be kind too. Mostly.

'My dad's got this mega promotion at work and he's going to make *heaps* more money. He's giving a big grown-up party for *his* friends this weekend and so *next* week, on Friday, the end of term, he says *I* can have a party too, so there. It's going to be a-maz-ing. So, who wants to come?'

The Girl Gang put their hands up. So did Sam and Richard. And most of the other girls in our class. But not Amy or Bella or Emily or me.

Chloe ignored us and shook her head pityingly at Sam and Richard.

'Sorry, guys. I'm not allowed to have boys at a sleepover,' she said.

Sam and Richard looked crestfallen.

'But maybe you could come for the party part and then go home?' Chloe suggested.

They perked up considerably.

'Awesome!' said Sam.

I don't like any of the boys much, but Sam is OK. He can be funny sometimes. Quite cheeky too, but Mrs Graham rarely tells him off. She usually says, 'Now that's enough, Sam!' in a fond way.

'And I suppose you could come to the Blue Door club too,' said Chloe, pausing for effect.

A gasp went round the class. The Blue Door club was famous. Even I'd heard of it, though we'd only moved here last term. It's a little bit like the leisure centre but apparently much much more glamorous. A famous actress and several footballers' wives hang out there and go to the gym and the spa. There's a huge midnight-blue swimming pool with marble pillars and silver lights all over the ceiling like indoor stars. I've seen a photo of it in a magazine.

'You're going swimming in the pool at the Blue Door?' Bella said in awe.

Bella loves swimming. She's very good at it. I saw lots of her trophies and certificates when I went to her sleepover. She goes to the leisure centre for training before school sometimes and attends a

special swimming club too. I quite like swimming but nowhere near as much as Bella.

'Yeah, the amazing midnight-blue swimming pool. Dad's reserving it specially for me and my friends,' said Chloe.

The Girl Gang all squealed. Sam and Richard high-fived each other.

'Can I come too?' Alfie asked.

'And me? And my mates?' Sanjad begged.

'Don't let the boys come too, they'll only muck about,' said Amelie, the leader of the Girl Gang. That started a big argument, girls versus boys.

'I've always longed to swim in the Blue Door pool,' said Bella.

Chloe smiled unpleasantly. 'I'm afraid it's dead exclusive, Bella. You can only go there if you're a member. Or a member's special guest. *I* can take

whoever I like.' She paused. 'Want to come?'

Bella blinked. Amy and Emily and I looked at her. Bella didn't look back at us.

'Yes please,' she said.

Chapter Three

We couldn't believe it.

'Bella!' Amy hissed, shocked. 'You can't go to Chloe's sleepover party. We're not friends with her any more.'

'I don't want to go to the sleepover. Or the party part either. But I'm desperate to swim in the Blue Door pool,' whispered Bella.

'Chloe's probably only playing one of her

famous jokes on you,' I said. 'You know what she's like. She's getting you all excited about it, but then she'll say she didn't really mean it and you can't come.'

I looked over at Chloe. Her blue eyes were glittering in a very witchy way. I think that was *exactly* what she wanted to do. She saw me glaring at her. She refreshed her smile.

'It will be great if you can come, Bella,' she cooed. 'You're so good at swimming. Maybe you can give us some tips?'

'Yeah, of course,' said Bella. She'd been lounging at her desk, her feet resting on Amy's chair, but now she sat up straight. 'And I could give diving lessons too, if you want.'

'You're really sucking up now!' Amy sneered.

'Don't *you* want to learn to dive, Amy? I thought

you had a crush on Tom Daley?' Bella said.

'I wouldn't want to go to Chloe's party even if Tom Daley himself was doing the teaching,' said Amy. 'You know perfectly well that Chloe's our worst enemy now.'

'Yeah, well, she used to be our friend until Daisy came to our school,' said Bella.

'Bella!' said Emily.

'And you were happy enough to be Chloe's best friend for ever before Daisy started hanging around you,' Bella retorted.

'Exactly,' said Chloe. 'So OK, that's you definitely coming, Bella. And Sam and Richard are *half* coming. So who else shall I pick?'

'Me!' the Girl Gang squealed. They'd been banking on coming because they were now officially Chloe's best friends. But it seemed Chloe intended

them to beg and plead like the rest of the class.

'Pick us!' someone said.

'Pick me, Chloe!'

'Please can I come? *Me!*' someone else shouted.

'Hey, hey, what's all this silly noise?' said Mrs Graham, bustling into the room. 'Sorry I'm late for registration. I had to take Bethany to the sickroom and phone her mother. She's not very well. But I didn't expect the whole class to start trumpeting like elephants in my absence.'

There were a few titters. Sam put his arm to his face, waving it around like an elephant's trunk. I couldn't help giggling.

'That's enough, Sam,' said Mrs Graham. 'All take your seats, children. That includes you, Chloe, unless you've decided to teach the class today instead of me?'

Chloe danced back to her desk in her high heels.

'Ah! Divine shoes, Chloe, though I fear you'll be hobbling around with bunions and hammer toes when you get to my age if you continue wearing them. But don't worry, I'm sure there are several pairs of comfy lace-ups in the lost property cupboard. Pop along at once and change into them, dear,' she said.

Chloe didn't pop along at once. She stood her ground in her pretty shoes, looking outraged.

'I can't wear someone else's manky old shoes!' she protested.

Mrs Graham changed her tone. 'Go at once, Chloe,' she said in such a steely manner that Chloe fled the classroom. I wondered whether I could ever adopt that kind of tone.

'*Stop bullying everyone and showing off about your*

stupid sleepover, Chloe, or I'll tell everyone how you disgraced yourself at my home!' I rehearsed it inside my head, but I knew I didn't dare say it straight to her face. It was very uncomfortable realizing I was such a complete wimp.

'I can't *believe* Bella could change her mind about Chloe just so she can go to her party,' Emily hissed to me.

'I know. She's really betrayed us,' I whispered back, though I couldn't feel totally furious with Bella. I knew how much she loved swimming. I could see why she couldn't bear to miss a chance of trying out the Blue Door pool. I badly wanted to see the marble pillars and the starry ceiling and the midnight-blue pool myself. Perhaps I could have begged Chloe to let me come to her sleepover party, but I knew she'd never invite me in a million years.

Chloe went on and on about her wretched Best Sleepover in the World at break and lunchtime. She couldn't do a little dance and go 'Ta dah!' wearing someone's ratty old black lace-ups with one of the soles flapping loose. She sat on her knees in the playground to hide the borrowed shoes.

'That Mrs Graham will be for it if I catch

verrucas!' Chloe muttered darkly, and then concentrated on leaking more information about her party, drip by drip, slowly working the whole class into a frenzy.

Emily, Amy and I decided to take no notice whatsoever. We even put our hands over our ears when she raised her voice.

Bella didn't know what to do. She usually sat with us and shared her chocolate, and we chatted and joked and had fun. She could still have joined us. It would have been awkward, but she was still *Bella*.

'Do you want to go and fetch her, Amy?' I asked, watching Bella standing awkwardly by herself in the middle of the playground.

'I think she's going to stand over there with Chloe and all that sickening slurpy lot telling Chloe

she's marvellous just because they want to be picked for her sleepover,' said Amy, still very angry.

Actually, Bella didn't go and stand near Chloe either. She wandered over to the other end of the playground and sat down with her back to the railings. She ate her whole chocolate bar herself.

'Poor Bella,' I said. I felt bad. She'd only been telling the truth. Chloe would still be best friends with Emily if I hadn't come along. And now it looked as if Amy and Bella were splitting up too, yet they'd been friends ever since they were at nursery school together.

I worried about it all day, though Emily did her best to reassure me.

'I never wanted to be Chloe's best friend in the first place, Daisy. She *chose* me and there was nothing I could do about it. I'm much happier being best friends with you. You know that,' she said.

I *did* know that, but I couldn't quite be sure. It was a relief when Mum came to collect me from school. That was our special time together. Dad was out at work. Lily didn't arrive home in her school bus until quarter past four. So Mum and I could walk home, and she'd have a cup of coffee, I'd have a glass of milk and we'd both have a chocolate teacake or a wafer bar. We could never make up our minds which was our favourite.

'Did you have a good day at school, darling?' Mum asked, as we were munching away.

I didn't really want to spoil the moment by telling her that Chloe was having an amazing sleepover party and I wasn't invited, and Bella and Amy had split up and it might be partly my fault.

I just shrugged and muttered that it was OK. Then I went and leaned against Mum and said I had a tummy ache. It wasn't actually a fib – my tummy really was hurting. Mum pulled me onto her lap and gave me a cuddle. She doesn't often do that now because I'm getting older and she's usually busy with Lily. It felt good.

Nor did I tell Dad about Chloe, though I knew he'd be sympathetic. He can't stand Chloe either and calls her a spoilt little madam.

The only person I told was Lily.

Chapter Four

I waited until we were both in bed. We don't share
a bedroom. Lily has a lovely big bedroom. I don't
mind. Lily is the elder sister after all. Plus she has
loads of extra stuff: a large bed that can be raised up
and down, a hoist to help her get in and out of bed,
a space for her wheelchair, plus a specially installed
little shower room and loo.

She has some fun stuff too, of course – her old

teddies, her musical box, her special tablet so she can stream music and listen to stories. She used not to be able to use anything herself. Mum or Dad did it for her. I did too. Lily always seemed to like it when it was my turn.

But now she's at her new special school she's having heaps of physio and her fingers work a little bit better, so she's learning to switch things on herself, though she still has to have a lot of help. The best thing of all is that she's learned to speak!

Well, she mostly says, 'Ur ur ur,' though sometimes I know exactly what she means. She's very clever, because she can speak *two* languages. She's been taught a special sign language called Makaton at her school.

I tried to learn sign language for deaf people once, so our old Alphabet Club could talk to each

other without anyone knowing what we were saying. The Alphabet Club was my idea when I made friends with Emily, Amy and Bella and had to be friends with horrible Chloe too. The first letters of our names are ABCDE. I thought this was a very clever idea for a club, but Chloe said she thought it was pathetic. She couldn't be bothered to learn the deaf alphabet and said I really had some nerdy ideas. Typical.

Makaton is fun because you act it too, and use symbols as well as signing. It's a bit of a struggle for Lily because her arms are a bit wobbly and she can't always make them do what she wants, but she tries ever so hard. Mum and Dad and I are learning it too. I suppose *we're* like a little club. If we go together to Morelli's, our favourite Italian restaurant down the road, Lily can silently sign when she wants a

drink or her mouth wiping, or she needs to go to the toilet, then no one else needs to know. Mrs Morelli doesn't mind a bit that Lily's wheelchair takes up a lot of room in her little restaurant.

Makaton is also very useful when I creep into Lily's bedroom at night. Especially on *this* night, when I couldn't get to sleep. Mum always switches her main light off, but Lily's teddy night light is left on. He's a cute little bear who shines in the dark. His eyes are shut, but I used to tell Lily that when she fell asleep he'd wake up. He'd jump onto her bed and use her duvet like a trampoline, bouncing up and down on his four tiny paws. She'd laugh and laugh.

Lily was wide awake when I went into her bedroom, which was good. Sometimes she gets startled if you wake her up and starts shouting.

I'd be in big trouble if Mum heard because it can take ages to get Lily back to sleep. She smiled now in the golden glow from her teddy night light and waved her hand once to say hello.

I waved hello back to her and I brushed my lips with my fingers. It's the sign for 'flower'. Lily signed 'flower' back to me. It's our nickname for each other as she's called Lily and I'm called Daisy. Then I held

out my arms enquiringly and Lily held up her closed fist, which means 'yes'. So I climbed into her big bed and put my arms round her. She struggled to brush her fingertips against the palm of her other hand. I knew that word: *Happy!*

Then she pointed to me. I hesitated. I didn't want to whine on to Lily about my problems. She had enough problems of her own without taking on any of my silly worries. Kids can sometimes be awful when we're out at the shops or in the park. They point at Lily and say horrible stuff. I always want to slap them when they're mean about her.

Mum takes no notice and says some children can't help being ignorant. I think Dad feels more like me, though of course he'd never actually slap anyone. I might. I'm a big wuss when it comes to standing up for myself, but I feel as fierce as a tiger

when people are hateful to Lily.

I can't even stand it when people are trying to be nice but say in hushed voices, 'Oh, poor little pet,' when they see Lily in her wheelchair. Don't they realize Lily has ears that work perfectly? She doesn't want to be pitied. I wonder if there's a Makaton sign for 'bog off'?

Anyway, I pointed to myself and signed that I was happy too, but then I started going all trembly.

'Actually, I'm not really happy,' I confessed, and buried my head in Lily's neck.

'Ur ur ur,' she said very softly. I don't think she was trying to say any specific words. She was simply being sympathetic.

'It's Chloe. *Again*,' I said. 'She's having another sleepover. She's called it the Best Sleepover in the World, would you believe? Though it does sound as

if it's going to be very special. She's taking people to this ultra-swanky Blue Door club where they have this awesome swimming pool. And of course I'm not invited because we're worst enemies. Not that I'm the slightest bit upset about that. But Bella is going. And now Amy isn't talking to her and it's spoiling everything. And what if Amy changes her mind and wants to go to Chloe's sleepover too?' I wailed. 'What if I never ever get invited to another sleepover party ever again?'

Lily was quiet for a moment. Makaton is great but it's not very complex. You can't express lots and lots.

She put two fingers together and pointed to herself, asking me to look at her. So I hitched myself up on one elbow and watched her pat her chest again, put her hands together at the side of her face

and close her eyes. That means 'sleep'. I thought she meant 'I'm going to sleep', but now she was signing something else, jiggling her hands up and down.

'Sorry?' I said.

Lily sighed impatiently and signed, 'You my sleep party.'

'What? You're asking me to *your* sleepover?' I asked.

Lily nodded again and again, clasping her hand and shaking it forward.

'Yes, yes, yes,' she signed.

Chapter Five

I thought Lily was simply trying to comfort me. I felt much better, though I was still a bit sniffly. We both went to sleep and didn't wake up until Mum came into Lily's room to help her get up.

'Hello, girls!' she said.

I thought Mum might tell me off, but she was smiling.

'Have you been having a little chat together?'

she asked, sitting at the foot of the bed and giving us both a pat.

Lily signed yes and went 'ur ur ur' for emphasis. Then she signed again. Mum struggled to understand.

'Party sleep?' she said. 'You two have been having a party in bed?'

We both laughed.

'I hope you haven't been giving Lily chocolate or crisps, Daisy?' she asked. 'You know she could easily choke if she's lying flat on her back.'

'*Yes*, Mum, of course I know,' I said.

Lily was busy signing 'sleep' and 'party' again and again.

'Sleepover!' Mum suddenly got it. 'Oh, girls. Not again. You've already *had* a sleepover, Daisy.'

Lily signed 'party sleep' for the umpteenth time

43

and thumped herself on the chest.

'*You* want a sleepover party, Lily?' said Mum. 'Oh, darling, it's a lovely idea but I don't think we could really manage it. Maybe if it's just Emily. I know you like her, Lily.'

Lily signed yes, and then thumped her chest again and clasped one hand with the other. I knew that sign.

'Friend!' I said.

Lily shouted in triumph.

Dad came into the bedroom in his pyjamas. 'Hello, all my girls,' he said. 'What are you yelling about, Lily? Can't your old dad have a little bit of a lie-in when he's on a late shift?'

'Lily wants to have a sleepover,' I said. 'Her own one.'

'Well, I don't see why not,' said Dad. 'As long as

she doesn't invite that little minx Chloe. She was a right pain at your last sleepover, Daisy.'

Dad put his hand on his hip, tossed his head as if he had long curls and made his mouth go pouty. It was a pretty good imitation of Chloe, which made us giggle. Then he clutched himself as if he was desperate for a wee, and that made Lily and me laugh hysterically, though Mum frowned.

'Which friend do you want to come, Lily? It *is* Emily, isn't it?' I asked.

Lily signed 'my friend' and pointed to her new bead bracelet. Mum had been worried when she came home from school wearing it. She'd phoned Lily's teacher, Jen, and asked her about it, saying she didn't think it was a very good idea because it could easily break and Lily might swallow a bead. Mum fusses way too much. Lily isn't a *baby*.

Jen told Mum that the bracelet was a present from Lily's friend Natalie. Mum hadn't heard of a Natalie at Lily's school. She wasn't one of the five children who travelled with Lily in the school bus. She wasn't in Lily's group. They were Shakura, Mandy, Jojo, Saul and Georgie. Lily always pulled a face when Georgie was mentioned. He mucked about a lot and wouldn't do as he was told. Dad

teased Lily that Georgie was her boyfriend, which made her furious.

'Who do you want to come to your sleepover then, Lily?' Dad asked. 'It's Georgie, isn't it?'

Lily tapped on one hand with two fingers from the other. She did it with emphasis. She was obviously signing '*Dad!*' Then she showed us her bracelet again.

'She wants Natalie to come,' I said. 'Is she your best friend now, Lily?'

She didn't need to sign. Her whole face lit up. I was so happy for Lily. I knew how much it meant to have a best friend.

'Then let's have her over for your sleepover,' said Dad. 'We'll phone Jen and get Natalie's mum's number. When would you like your sleepover, Princess Lily?'

Lily poked her cheek twice with her finger. I knew that meant 'Easy!' She poked again, so I suppose she was saying 'Easy-peasy!' Then she looked at me.

'Next Friday,' I said.

Mum frowned. 'Why not have your sleepover on a Saturday, darling? Next Friday's the last day of school, so everything will be a bit hectic. Saturday would be much better – or indeed *any* day in the holidays?'

Lily signed 'No!' very firmly indeed. She looked at me again.

'She says it absolutely has to be next Friday. Please. Pretty please? With a cherry on the top?'

I said, and Lily said, 'Yes, yes, yes,' by rocking her closed fist backwards and forwards.

'Oh, girls, don't gang up on me. Let me think about it,' said Mum. 'Come on, Lily, let's get you up and sorted. You go and get washed and dressed too, Daisy, quick sharp.'

I was very quick and extra sharp, and in ten minutes I was downstairs in my uniform. I'd even done my plaits, sort of. I started laying the table for breakfast to be extra helpful so that Mum would say yes.

Mum and Lily take much longer because Lily can't wash herself or put her own clothes on. Dad came down to the kitchen long before them and started making tea and toast.

'OK, what's going on with you and Lily?' he asked. 'Whose idea was the sleepover? And why

does it absolutely have to be next Friday?'

'Just because,' I said.

'Daisy?' Dad said softly. 'Come on, talk to your old dad.'

'Because Chloe's having the Best Sleepover in the World and she hasn't asked me to come, but now Bella's going though I thought she didn't like Chloe any more, and Amy might go too, even though she says she won't, and I'm scared Emily might too, though I know she won't really because she's my best friend for ever and – and – and—' I gabbled.

'Hey, hey, calm down, sweetheart,' said Dad, giving me a hug.

I snuggled into his shirt, breathing in his warm, safe Dad-smell. He patted me on the back.

'So you told Lily all this?' he said. 'And she wants

a sleepover on the same day so you can come to it and won't feel so sad about that awful Chloe child?'

'I think so,' I said.

'Bless her!' said Dad, and for a second his voice went a bit wobbly. 'You two special girls.'

When I looked up I saw his eyes were watery. The toaster pinged and four slices of toast popped up, making us both jump.

'What do you want on your toast, Daisy? Strawberry jam? Honey? Marmalade? Peanut butter? Ice cream? Shoe polish?' he asked.

'Dad!' I said, giggling.

'That's better,' said Dad, giving me a little tap on the end of my nose.

'Ping!' I said, just like the toaster.

'Do you know what, Daisy? Chloe's got it all wrong,' said Dad. 'She can't possibly be having the

best sleepover in the world because you and Lily are going to have the Absolutely, Definitely Best Sleepover in the Entire World!'

Chapter Six

I told Emily about Lily's sleepover the second I got
to school.

'Oh, that's great, Daisy!' she said. 'Can I come?'

'Of *course*, Em. It'll be you, me, Lily and this new
friend of hers from her school,' I said.

'So is she like Lily? You know, not very good at
walking and talking?' Emily asked a little awkwardly.

'I suppose so. I haven't met her yet. But she

sounds nice. She gave Lily a friendship bracelet,'
I said.

'We'll have to make ourselves friendship
bracelets,' said Emily.

'Fantastic!' I said. I felt like making Emily a
friendship necklace too, and friendship rings, and
friendship earrings, even though we weren't allowed
to have our ears pierced. She was the best friend in
all the world.

Amy was hovering, looking rather lost.

'You could come to Lily's sleepover too, Amy.
That would be great,' I said.

'Thank you,' said Amy. She looked so lost
without Bella.

'I'll ask Bella too if you like. Maybe she'd sooner
come to Lily's sleepover than Chloe's,' I suggested,
though I thought it highly unlikely.

Bella was sitting on top of her desk by herself, nibbling her chocolate bar.

I waved to her. 'Hey, Bella!' I called.

She lifted her arm in a half-wave, looking uncomfortable. She might have come over, but Chloe came charging into the classroom. Her gang crowded around her.

'Hey, you guys, listen up,' she said. 'You'll never ever guess what!'

'I can't stand it when she says stuff in that silly voice,' I said to Emily and Amy. I couldn't say it to Bella because she'd gone over to Chloe too – *and was sharing her chocolate bar with her.*

'I can't stick Chloe, full stop,' said Amy miserably. She kept looking over at Bella.

'Do you wish you and Bella were still friends?' I asked.

'No. I can't stick her either,' said Amy, but I don't think she really meant it.

'Shut up, you lot, and listen!' said Chloe. 'We're going to do the Prance Dance at my sleepover.'

'Well, so what?' said Emily. 'We can do the Prance Dance whenever we want.'

I felt like hugging her. She was such a lovely, loyal friend.

'Yeah, so what?' said Amy, but she looked a little envious. She loves dancing. We can't really do the Prance Dance properly in the playground because the boys tease us, even Sam. Richard doesn't tease. He joins in too. He's actually better at dancing than the other girls, even Amy.

'Yes, but you can't do the Prance Dance *with Mattie Rayburn*. She's actually coming to my sleepover, would you believe!' said Chloe. She stood

with her hands on her hips, waiting for the reaction. She got it. Everyone screamed. Even Amy.

Mrs Graham came into the classroom, her cup of coffee in her hand. 'For goodness' sake, what's the

matter with you? I could hear you all the way from the staffroom,' she said. 'Stop this silly screaming! Why can't you be trusted to talk *quietly* to your friends before school starts? The next person who speaks will be sent to Miss Raynor!'

Everyone was quiet as a mouse because Miss Raynor is our head teacher and she's ancient and very strict. But everyone's eyes were

still popping at Chloe's news. Chloe herself sat demurely at her desk, her cheeks pink. People kept passing her little notes but she didn't take any notice. She simply sat there smugly, letting everyone else simmer.

They clamoured round her at break time, quacking questions like a flock of ducks.

'She's winding everyone up. She just means she'll put that Mattie Rayburn video on her gigantic television,' said Amy. 'That's what my sisters do. We dance together. I can do that any time at home.'

'Well, we can do that at my house at Lily's sleepover,' I said quickly. 'She can't dance but I could help her jiggle her arms about. And help her friend Natalie too.' I knew I shouldn't try to take over Lily's sleepover. But I was desperate not to lose any more of my friends. It was such a shock to see

Bella cosying up to Chloe. Still, at least Amy wasn't going to be tempted away. Or so I thought.

'Of course it's not going to be us showing Mattie's video,' Chloe said scornfully. 'She's coming to my house and going to dance *in person*.'

'She's fibbing. Mattie Rayburn couldn't possibly be coming to her house!' said Amy. 'Mattie Rayburn's massive. She gets like a gazillion followers.'

'Yeah, and my dad's firm is doing a deal with her people to produce a whole range of Mattie Rayburn leisurewear,' said Chloe triumphantly. 'And as she's doing a signing on Friday to promote her *Girls Have Fun* book, she's coming afterwards to my sleepover party. There'll be a film crew recording to show Mattie dancing with her fans. That's us! So there! Bet you wish you were coming to my sleepover now, Amy? I *told* you it was going to be the

Best Sleepover in the Entire World.'

Amy said nothing. She just blinked at Chloe.

'Couldn't Amy come, Chloe?' said Bella.

Chloe shrugged. 'Maybe. If she asks nicely.'

'Please, please, please,' Bella begged.

Please, please, please don't say yes, I said inside my head.

Amy looked at me. She mouthed one word. 'Sorry!' Then she walked over to Chloe.

'Please can I come to your sleepover party, Chloe?' she said.

'Of course you can come,' said Chloe. 'After all, you and Bella are my oldest friends. And what about you, Emily? Want to come too?'

I started trembling.

'Sorry!' said Emily. I think she was trembling too. 'I've said I'm going to Daisy's sister's party.'

'You'll be *sorrrryyyy*,' said Chloe, folding her arms and shaking her head.

Chapter Seven

Emily and I went off by ourselves.

'Chloe's only trying to wind you up,' I said.

'Who cares,' said Emily boldly.

I knew she did care. She'd been friends with Amy and Bella long before me. And she was Chloe's *best* friend. If it wasn't for me she'd be all set to swim under the stars in the midnight blue-pool and do the Prance Dance with Mattie Rayburn.

For the first time ever we ran out of things to say to each other. There were squeals coming from the far side of the playground. Chloe was demonstrating the Prance Dance while a dozen girls tried to copy her. Emily was watching them, though she looked away quickly when she saw I'd noticed.

I swallowed. 'You can go if you want,' I muttered.

'What?' said Emily.

'Go to her sleepover. I won't mind,' I said, though of course I minded terribly.

'Don't be daft,' said Emily. 'I'd sooner go to Lily's sleepover.'

'It's ever so kind of you to pretend,' I said, my throat so dry I could barely speak.

'I'm not pretending,' Emily insisted. 'We'll have way more fun, you and me and Lily and her friend.'

We *would* have fun at Lily's sleepover, wouldn't

we? Though what exactly would we *do*, the four of us?

I worried about it the rest of the day. I couldn't concentrate properly during lessons and got told off twice by Mrs Graham because I couldn't answer questions.

'Do you want to come and play tomorrow?' Emily asked. 'I've got some beads. We could make our own friendship bracelets.'

'I would love to,' I said, but when I asked Mum she shook her head.

'I'm sorry, Daisy. We're going to see Granny and Grandad on Saturday – don't you remember?' said Mum.

'But we can see them any old time,' I said. 'Please, can't I go to Emily's?'

'Another time, darling,' said Mum.

'But it's really important,' I said. 'I need to make friendship bracelets with Emily so we can stay best friends.'

'You don't need bracelets to be friends, silly,' said Mum.

'You don't *understand*,' I wailed. 'I'm scared she'll go to Chloe's sleepover after all, especially now Mattie Rayburn herself is going to do the Prance Dance.'

'Who?' said Mum. She's a big fan of *Strictly* but she doesn't know anything about the latest dance crazes. She'd clearly never even heard of Mattie Rayburn. Well, I had only got to know about her recently. And I didn't actually have a clue how to do the Prance Dance, so I couldn't do it with Emily at Lily's sleepover.

I sighed deeply.

'Come on, don't go sulky on me, Daisy,' said Mum. 'Tell me about this Prance Dance thingy.'

'There's no point,' I snapped. 'Mum, what are we going to *do* at Lily's sleepover?'

'I don't know,' said Mum. 'I've been racking my brains. I don't know what Natalie's needs are. I'm not sure her mum will say yes. And where will she sleep? I don't think sleeping bags in a tent would work. I don't even know how Lily and Natalie can play any games. It was sweet of Lily to suggest a sleepover, but it's not really practical. I just hope Lily's forgotten about it.'

I gave Mum a look. Mum doesn't always *get* Lily. She *never* forgets.

She gave Mum and me a huge smile when Jeff the school driver edged her wheelchair up our garden path. Lily waved to him and signed 'hello' to us. She was clutching an envelope.

'Is this from school?' asked Mum.

Lily clasped her hand and rocked it forward, making little squeals of excitement. Mum opened the envelope, looking anxious. It was a beautifully typed letter – but it was signed *Natalie*. It was a rather wobbly signature, but perfectly clear.

The letter said: 'I'd love to come to Lily's sleepover next Friday. It will be BRILLIANT. My mum's address, phone number and email are at the top of the page. I like to eat everything, especially CAKE. Love from Natalie.'

Jeff had started up the school bus by this time, but Mum left Lily and me and ran to catch him. She tapped on his window and he wound it down.

'Hang on, Jeff. Can you tell me, do you know Natalie?' Mum asked hurriedly.

'Of course I know Natalie. I drop her off home before your Lily,' said Jeff. 'Right little character, she is.'

'She's written a letter saying she's coming to us next Friday,' said Mum.

'That's right. She's ever so excited about your Lily's sleepover. They've only recently palled up but now they're thick as thieves, bless them.' He waved to Lily in her wheelchair, still at the front door. She gave him a thumbs-up sign. He did a thumbs-up sign back to her and then drove off.

As soon as Mum had wheeled Lily inside, she gave us both juice and a banana in the kitchen and then hurried into the living room and shut the door. I mashed Lily's banana and added brown sugar. I dipped my banana straight into the sugar bag.

'Don't tell!' I said to Lily, and winked at her. I helped her eat and she munched happily, sucking her straw after every mouthful.

'I bet you Mum's phoning your friend Natalie's mum,' I said.

Lily nodded her hand to say yes.

'Did she really type that letter herself?' I asked.

Lily nodded again and then drew her thumb across her forehead. I knew that sign! Mum was always doing it to Lily, and then touching her finger to her cheek, which means 'clever girl'.

'So Natalie's clever,' I said. 'And so are you. It's so cool you've got a best friend now and so have I.'

I felt so happy. Of course we'd have fun together – and eat lots of cake. It was sad that Bella and Amy were new recruits to Chloe's gang but that couldn't be helped. Chloe's party might prove to be the best sleepover in all the world but *I* still had the best friend in all the world – and the best sister too. I dug my finger in the brown sugar bag and sucked it happily.

Lily thumped her chest, so I gave her a fingerful of sugar too. Mum came into the kitchen and caught us but she didn't get cross.

'You're a pair of greedy guts,' she said, putting the sugar bag on the top shelf in the cupboard, too high for me to reach. She seemed very smiley.

'I've just been speaking to Natalie's mum,' she said.

'Told you so,' I murmured to Lily.

'She sounds lovely,' said Mum. She tapped the tip of Lily's nose. 'I'm so glad you've made friends with Natalie, darling.'

Lily gave her thumbs-up sign again and stroked her friendship bracelet proudly.

Chapter Eight

We drove to Granny and Grandad's on Saturday. We have a very weird car – well, I suppose it's more of a van. It has to be really roomy because we need space for Lily's wheelchair in the back. There's not actually much space for me. I've got a little seat beside her. Lily feels fine when we drive, but I nearly always feel sick.

Lily looked at me and clenched her fists, her little

fingers in the air, making a perfect sign for 'ill'. I nodded and signed 'ill' myself, sticking my tongue out at the side of my mouth to be silly. I was starting to feel I'd have to beg Dad to stop driving so I could leap out and throw up, but just in time we turned into Granny and Grandad's road.

'Here we are!' Mum said, determinedly bright.

I struggled out and leaned weakly on the side of the van, taking deep gulps of fresh air. There was a big kerfuffle getting the ramp in place and Lily in her wheelchair down it. Granny kept saying, 'Careful with the poor little pet!' to Mum and Dad, as if she thought they'd give Lily a good shove and send her wheelchair hurtling down like a toboggan.

Then Granny was all over Lily, kissing her and tickling her under the chin, using a special coochy-coo voice. I hate the way she treats Lily like a baby.

Lily hates it too. Granny made a fuss of me as well, but she pinched my cheeks and shook her head at me.

'Dear goodness, you're white as a sheet, Daisy. What's the matter with you?' she said.

'I feel a bit travel sick, that's all, Granny,' I said.

Granny sighed as if she thought I was feeling sick on purpose. 'You need to run about in the fresh air and get some roses in your cheeks. Count your blessings!' she said.

I pulled a face at her when she turned her back. Mum saw and frowned. Dad also saw and grinned sympathetically. He finds Granny hard work too.

Grandad's OK though. He doesn't say much but he sings funny songs sometimes, and slips Lily and me squares of chocolate when he thinks no one's looking. He loves chocolate almost as much as Bella.

Best of all, Uncle Gary was there too! He's Mum's much younger brother, the coolest uncle in the world. We so love it when Uncle Gary comes visiting at the same time as us. He's brilliant with Lily. 'Our little flowery princess on her throne!' he said, sweeping into a daft curtsy that made her giggle.

'And darling Princess Daisy too!' he said, opening his arms wide.

I gave him a big hug. He calls Lily and me his special girls. He stayed talking to us in the living room while Dad went into the garden to chat to Grandad about his roses, and Mum went into the kitchen to help Granny with the lunch.

'Do you know what we're having, Uncle Gary?' I asked, not sure I liked the smell so soon after feeling sick.

'Rack of lamb rubbed with mustard and cooked with Greek beans,' Uncle Gary whispered.

I pulled a face. I hated eating lamb because I always thought of little white fluffy creatures gambolling in fields, and I wasn't sure I'd like Greek beans.

'I'm not feeling enthusiastic either,' Uncle Gary murmured. 'I'm not sure I'll manage to chomp away heartily. I had a very late night staying on at the

club. In fact, I didn't get back till this morning.'
Uncle Gary slapped himself on the back of his hand.
'Naughty boy!' he joked.

Lily chuckled and made the sign for 'naughty',
wagging her littlest finger twice.

'That's Lily saying you're naughty too,' I said.

'Wow, Lily, your signing's really cool,' said Gary.
'You're going to have to teach me. I could introduce
it into my act, like a mime artist.'

Uncle Gary works in a nightclub. At night,
obviously. He dresses up as a lady. I've never been
allowed to see his act but I'm sure he's brilliant.

'I wish you were here every time we come to
Granny's, Uncle Gary,' I said.

Lily made her clasped hand nod in agreement.

'I know, my darlings. I like a lie-in on a Saturday
– but I like my two princesses even more,' said

Uncle Gary, blowing us both a kiss.

'You could come round to our house, so it could be just us,' I suggested. 'It would be much more fun.'

'Ooh! Shh! We don't want the Queen Bee to hear and get upset, do we?' said Uncle Gary, glancing towards the kitchen.

Lily didn't have to be told to lower her voice. She could sign silently. She pointed to Uncle Gary, she pointed to herself, and then made the sign for 'sleep party'.

'*Yes!*' I shouted, and then clapped my hand over my mouth.

Granny came charging into the living room, her fluffy pink mules flapping on the floor. Granny was flapping too.

'What's all the shouting, Daisy? Gary, are you getting the girls overexcited? What's the matter,

Lily, you poor little pet?' Granny said. 'Look, she's gone dribbly.'

'Lily's fine,' said Mum, quickly giving Lily's chin a quick wipe with the special flannel tucked beside her in the wheelchair.

Lily frowned, embarrassed.

'Her mouth's simply watering because of the lovely smells coming from the kitchen,' said Uncle Gary. 'Rack of lamb, eh! And baked beans!'

'They're special giant beans in a home-cooked tomato sauce, not bog-standard baked beans out of a tin,' said Granny, not realizing he was winding her up.

'More's the pity,' he murmured. Then he raised his voice and said, 'So are we going Greek for pudding too? I love baklava.' He was sucking up to Granny now, but she looked huffy.

'I was planning to make a special Greek custard tart, but it just so happens your father's made dessert today. He's got into baking now he's retired.'

'*Dad* has?' said Gary. 'I thought he was one of the old soldiers who couldn't even boil an egg.'

'He's got hooked on *Bake Off*,' said Granny.

'Seriously?' said Uncle Gary. 'Does he watch out for soggy bottoms?'

'Don't be rude,' said Granny, swatting at Gary with the tea towel.

'So is he any good at it?' Mum asked.

'Well, I suppose. Though he's such an old fuddy-duddy. He makes the sort of cakes that are hopelessly old-fashioned. Pineapple upside-down cake, treacle tart, blackcurrant cheesecake, that type of thing. He's made a Black Forest gateau for today, would you believe? So seventies!' said Granny, tutting.

'I didn't know you could get black cake,' I said. 'Like it's burnt?'

'Don't be silly, dear,' said Granny. 'One joker in the family is quite enough.'

I *was* being serious, but I didn't argue.

We were all quite full up when it came to pudding time. I'd eaten a lot of Greek beans and mashed potato (and only two mouthfuls of lamb), and was sure I'd only be able to manage a sliver of cake.

I changed my mind immediately when Grandad

proudly brought in his Black Forest gateau and set it in the middle of the table for everyone to admire. It was a huge chocolate sponge cake sandwiched together by three layers of chocolate cream, with gorgeous deep red cherries and whirls of more cream on the top.

'It's probably much too rich for the girls,' said Granny. 'In fact, Daisy shouldn't really have any as she wouldn't eat her meat up properly, and Lily might choke on a cherry, so perhaps don't serve her either.'

Lily and I protested bitterly in our different ways. We were allowed a small slice each – and it was sheer bliss. If Bella had a portion she'd practically explode with delight because she loved chocolate so much. And Amy. And Emily loved chocolate too.

I had a sudden idea. I turned to Lily. She was

looking at me too, her eyes bright. She cupped one hand on top of her other – and I guessed that meant 'cake'. Then she signed 'sleep party' and put both thumbs up. She'd obviously had exactly the same idea!

Chapter Nine

Grandad couldn't get the hang of Makaton so I asked him on Lily's behalf.

'Do you think you could possibly make another Black Forest gateau for Lily's sleepover party next Friday, Grandad?' I asked.

Grandad looked thrilled. 'Of course I can! It would be an absolute honour!' he said.

Granny looked put out. And Mum did too.

'I was going to make Lily a flower cake,' she said.
'You know, like the Daisy birthday cake I made for
you, Daisy.'

I looked at Lily. I could see what she'd prefer. Me
too. I thought quickly.

'My daisy cake was beautiful, Mum. I'm sure
Lily wants a lily cake for *her* birthday. But this isn't a
birthday, it's a *non*-birthday sleepover. And she loves
chocolate, don't you, Lily?'

Lily signed yes very enthusiastically.

'Well then, I'd be happy to make you one, lovie,'
said Grandad.

Granny rolled her eyes.

Mum watched a weepy film in the living room
with Granny in the afternoon. Grandad and Dad
loaded the dishwasher and then went off to watch
sport on the television in Grandad's den. Uncle Gary,

Lily and I hung out in the kitchen. Uncle Gary showed us little clips of cute kittens on his mobile and we all went 'Aaah!'

Then I asked him to show us Mattie Rayburn doing the Prance Dance.

'Really?' said Uncle Gary, pulling a face, but he showed us anyway. Mattie Rayburn looked amazing in a tiny pink top and pink shorts and pink shoes with heels. She did her signature dance, skipping and wiggling and tossing her head.

I sighed.

'What's this sudden interest in little Miss Rayburn?' Uncle Gary asked.

'She's going to Chloe's sleepover,' I said. 'Her dad's fixed it. She'll teach everyone the Prance Dance.'

'Well, lucky you!' said Uncle Gary, though he didn't sound as if he meant it.

'I'm not invited,' I said.

'Ah!' said Uncle Gary. 'So you're not friends with this Chloe any more?'

'She doesn't like me one bit. In fact, I'm her worst enemy,' I said.

'Are some of your friends going to Chloe's sleepover?' Uncle Gary asked.

'Amy and Bella are. But Emily's not going. She's my best ever friend now, though she used to be

Chloe's best friend.'

'Oh, I get it,' said Uncle Gary.

Lily was watching me.

'I don't mind though,' I insisted. 'Because I'm going to Lily's sleepover that day and Emily's invited too, isn't she, Lily?'

Lily pointed to Uncle Gary.

'We want you to come too, Uncle Gary. You'd be our best ever guest,' I said, and Lily agreed.

'It's so sweet of you to invite me, girls. I wish I could come. But I have to work Friday evenings. It's the big night for me at the club,' said Uncle Gary.

'Oh,' I said, terribly disappointed.

'Ur ur ur,' said Lily, and she raised her hand and made a downwards sign in front of her nose.

'Are you signing "sad"?' Uncle Gary asked anxiously.

Lily closed her fist and nodded it. She wasn't just signing. Her eyes were watery.

'Oh, don't cry, darling, I can't bear it!' said Uncle Gary. He brought a lovely silk hankie out of his pocket and gently wiped Lily's face. It must have felt much nicer than her flannel.

'Listen, girls, what time is your sleepover?'

'We don't really know yet. Any time,' I said. 'But it would be almost the best sleepover in the world if you could come, Uncle Gary,' I said.

'Well, I'll have a chat with your mum and dad and see if I can come for part of it. Would that be OK?' Uncle Gary asked.

I nodded my head, Lily nodded her fist. It would be more than OK. It would be marvellous. I was sure Emily would love Uncle Gary. Lily was certain her friend Natalie would love him too.

I still wasn't quite sure what we would actually *do* though. I thought back to the other sleepovers I'd been to. We'd danced at Amy's sleepover – but Lily and Natalie couldn't dance. We'd played football at Emily's sleepover – but Lily and Natalie couldn't play football. We'd made pizzas at Chloe's first sleepover – but Lily and Natalie couldn't make pizzas (though they could certainly eat them). We'd slept in a tent at my sleepover but I didn't think Lily and Natalie could manage to lie in a sleeping bag.

I counted on my fingers. What other sleepover had I been to? Oh, Bella's! I didn't like thinking about Bella. If she hadn't said she'd go to Chloe's sleepover now, then Amy wouldn't have either and we'd still be in our proper foursome, all of us friends. The thought of the magical midnight-blue pool at the Blue Door had been just too tempting. We'd

gone swimming at the ordinary swimming baths at Bella's sleepover. Lily and Natalie couldn't go to the swimming baths at the leisure centre because they needed hoists to get them in and out. They had those at the pool at their special school.

That set me thinking. Maybe Lily *could* have a swim at her sleepover?

I thought about it on Sunday.

'Do you like swimming at your school, Lily?' I asked.

She nodded her hand enthusiastically for yes.

'And does Natalie like it too?'

Another yes.

'How about you have a swim with Natalie at your school on Friday after your lessons are finished – and

perhaps Emily and I could come too?' I suggested.

Lily signed, 'Yes, yes, yes!'

We asked Mum and Dad if they could arrange it with the school but they went, 'No, no, no!'

'Don't be so silly, Daisy,' said Mum. 'It's a therapy pool, not a leisure centre. And it's the last day of term. How could we possibly ask Jen or any of the other teachers to stay behind and supervise Lily and Natalie in the swimming pool? And what about

coming home? I suppose I could fetch Lily, but our car's not big enough to accommodate two wheelchairs. Do you seriously expect Jeff to wait an extra hour to drive you all back here?'

She was making it all so complicated! I looked at Dad pleadingly, but he shook his head too.

'It simply wouldn't be fair to ask, girls. Can't you see that?' Dad said.

We didn't want to see. We wanted to be upset. I moaned and groaned and said it wasn't fair. Lily had one of her turns. And guess what? I got the blame.

It was a bleak Sunday.

Chapter Ten

Monday was worse.

I got to school early and Emily was there too, which seemed great. I told her all about the trip to Granny and Grandad's and how Uncle Gary was coming to Lily's sleepover. I said how lovely and funny he was, and I went on about Grandad's Black Forest gateau, saying it was the best cake I'd ever tasted and I knew she'd think it delicious.

I went on and on. Emily didn't say very much. She mostly just nodded as she doodled on the back of her school jotter. She was drawing little flowers with lots of petals. I hoped they were daisies.

'Emily?' I said. 'You really will like Grandad's cake. It's really yummy.'

'Yes, it sounds lovely,' she said.

'And Uncle Gary is truly fantastic. I bet you'll wish he was your uncle when you meet him,' I said. 'He's ever so funny. And not like a boring grown-up at all. He's really kind.'

'Mmm,' said Emily.

Amy and Bella came into the classroom arm in arm. We stared at one another and then nodded awkwardly.

Amy and Bella hovered, and I wondered if they might come over. They looked as if they wanted to. But then Chloe came in, surrounded by her Girl Gang and Sam and Richard, each of them vying for her attention. Amy and Bella joined them. But Chloe shrugged them away and came over to Emily and me.

'Hi, Em,' she said, totally ignoring me.

'Hi,' Emily muttered, not looking up. She started on another daisy doodle. It went a bit lopsided because her hand was shaking.

'Wasn't it fun on Saturday?' said Chloe.

My heart started thumping.

Emily gave the tiniest nod, flushing pink. Her pen made a little blotch on the page.

'You're getting really good at football,' said Chloe.

I thought I was going to explode.

Emily gave a little shrug. Her face was painfully red now.

'Wasn't it funny when you scored a goal and your baby brother gave a screech as if he was cheering you,' said Chloe, laughing.

Emily didn't laugh. She looked as if she was going to cry.

'I think we'll have a big game of footie at my sleepover party,' said Chloe. 'That would be great, wouldn't it, Em?'

Emily didn't say yes. But she didn't say no either. She just started doodling another daisy as if her life depended on it.

'Hey, guys, what do you think? Shall we play football at my sleepover?' Chloe called to her gang. 'I'll have to make sure we're an even number. So,

two teams need twenty-two players. I could invite twenty-one friends. No, maybe twenty, because we'll ask Mattie Rayburn to join in too. What do you think?'

They were still cheering when Mrs Graham came into the room to start the morning lesson.

'Simmer down and go to your desks, everyone,' she said.

'It's not what you think,' Emily muttered to me desperately, and went to sit down.

I didn't know what to think. My whole head was thumping now. Chloe had obviously been at Emily's house on Saturday to play football. Emily had asked me round to make bracelets, but I couldn't go as we were visiting Granny and Grandad. So had Emily asked Chloe instead?

I couldn't believe it. Chloe was playing tricks on

me, only wanting to wind me up. But Emily hadn't denied it. She hadn't even looked at me. Maybe she was Chloe's best friend again and going to *her* sleepover party.

The first two lessons were misery. Chloe kept sending little paper messages to Emily. She saw me watching and waggled her nose at me, meaning I was being nosy. She whispered to Amy and Bella too. They seemed to be a best-friend foursome now, and I was totally left out.

When the bell rang for break time I made a bolt for the toilets and locked myself inside a cubicle, unable to bear the idea of having no one to go round with at playtime. I heard other girls clatter in and out. They were mostly talking about Chloe's sleepover. One said she was sure they were going to be driven in a fleet of limousines to and from the

Blue Door. Another said she'd heard they were all being given a makeover after their swim, which involved having their hair styled and their faces made up with lipstick, powder, blusher, even eyeliner and mascara.

I'd never been in a limousine and Mum said I was far too young for any kind of make-up. I was only allowed lip balm in the winter when my lips got chapped. It made my mouth glisten but it wasn't like real lipstick.

I had a little weep inside my cubicle, though I had to do it very quietly in case anyone heard me. I was still crying when I heard a voice calling me.

'Daisy? Daisy!' It was Emily. I wondered if Chloe and Amy and Bella were with her too. Had they heard me crying? Were they waiting silently, ready to have a good laugh at me when I emerged?

'Oh, Daisy, please come out!' Emily sounded desperate.

I wiped my eyes with the back of my hand and came out of the cubicle. Just Emily was there, peering at me anxiously.

'You've been crying!' she said at once.

'So?' I mumbled.

'Here. I've got a paper hankie,' said Emily, scrabbling up her sleeve. She mopped my face carefully and then gave me a hug. I stood still and stiff inside her arms for a moment, but then I couldn't help hugging her back.

'Are we still friends?' I whispered.

'Of course we are, you banana,' said Emily fondly.

'But you're Chloe's friend too now?' I said.

'No I'm not!' she protested.

'Didn't you invite her round to your house on Saturday?'

'I didn't. I swear I didn't. She came round with her mother, but I didn't *ask* her. They just knocked on our door. Her mum said to my mum that Chloe was very upset that we weren't friends any more and couldn't we make up. And I was going, "No, no, no!" Well, inside my head I was. My mum *knows* I'm your friend now, but she felt she had to be polite and so she invited them in. It was so *awkward.*'

'So you played football with Chloe?' I said.

'I didn't know what else I could do with her!' said Emily.

The bell went for the end of break time, making us both jump.

'Come on, we'd better go,' Emily said, but I still hesitated. I had to ask her. 'Emily, are you going to Chloe's sleepover now?'

'No, of course not,' said Emily – but she wasn't looking straight at me.

'You *are*!' I said.

'I am not, I promise. Well, she did ask me, but I'm not going. I'm going to Lily's sleepover – you know I am,' Emily gabbled. 'Daisy, Mrs Graham is going to be so cross if we're late.'

I let her pull me out of the girls' cloakrooms and along the corridor. I hung back just outside the classroom.

'Did Chloe's mum ask your mum if you could go to her rubbish sleepover?' I mumbled hurriedly.

'Well, yes, because I hadn't actually told her yet about Lily's sleepover, but it's all right. I've told her now and she says I can choose. So of course I choose you and Lily. Unless . . .' She hesitated. I waited to hear what was coming. I was so worked up I thought I might have to charge back to the cloakrooms to be sick.

Chapter Eleven

'Unless what?' I said to Emily.

'Well, Chloe says you can come too, truly. So if you wanted, we could both go together and get to swim in the Blue Door pool and meet Mattie Rayburn and do the Prance Dance and have a Little Princess makeover,' said Emily.

'But what about Lily's sleepover?'

'Couldn't she have her sleepover on another day?' Emily asked.

'No! It's all arranged,' I said. But already I was thinking we could actually have Lily's sleepover any day in the summer holidays. We just had to tell her friend Natalie there was a change of date. It wouldn't matter. Though would it matter to Lily? She'd understand, surely – wouldn't she?

'Couldn't we *re*arrange it?' Emily said.

Then Mrs Graham came storming out of the classroom.

'When you two have finished your little gossip perhaps you might care to come into the classroom so I can start the lesson,' she said acidly.

We went back in, everyone staring at us. Chloe's eyes were like lasers.

I wondered if she'd really said she'd invite me too. It was probably another trick. But what if I *could*

go? I would swim in the midnight-blue pool. I wouldn't know Mattie Rayburn if I bumped right into her, but I knew it would be something to show off about if I met her and I could learn this silly Prance Dance. I could have the Little Princess makeover. I wouldn't be left out. I would still be Emily's best friend.

Lily wouldn't mind if I changed the date of her sleepover. Uncle Gary might be able to come for longer then. Grandad could still make us his Black Forest gateau. And I was sure Natalie would be able to change the date. It was probably much more convenient to have the sleepover in the holidays. Mum had said so, hadn't she?

It was simple . . . wasn't it?

I passed a note to Emily in class.

OK, I'll come to Chloe's sleepover if you're really really sure she's not playing tricks on us.
Daisy xxx

She passed one back.

Great great great xxx

We went up to Chloe at lunchtime. We were both a bit trembly. We held hands for a moment. I wasn't sure if it was my hand that had gone all sweaty or Emily's. Maybe it was both.

Chloe was surrounded, as always.

'Chloe, can we have a little chat?' Emily asked.

Chloe looked at us. 'OK. A moment, you guys,' she said, dismissing everyone else in a queenly fashion.

I really, really, really couldn't stand Chloe. But I really, really, really wanted to go to her sleepover and keep Emily as my best friend for ever.

'Chloe, you know you told me Daisy can come to your sleepover too?' Emily said. 'Well, do you really mean it?'

We waited. Chloe's blue eyes were very bright, but she wasn't smiling. I tried to work out what she was thinking. She kept us waiting a long time. Then she shrugged.

'I expect so – though I'll have to ask my mum,' she said. 'There are way too many people wanting to come.'

'Yes, but Daisy really has to be invited or I won't be able to come either,' Emily said bravely.

'OK,' said Chloe, and then she sauntered back

to her little gang to tell them more about the Little Princess makeover.

'How about having a Little *Prince* makeover?' said Sam.

'Oh yes! Though could we still be made up?' Richard asked.

'Maybe,' said Chloe.

'I'm not allowed to wear make-up,' I said to Emily.

'Neither am I. Still, it won't matter if it's only for a party. And we could wash it off before we go home,' said Emily. 'Oh, Daisy, isn't it great that you can come too?'

'Yes it is,' I said, but it didn't really feel great somehow. 'Chloe hasn't actually *said* I can come, not properly.'

'Yes she has! When I mentioned it she said OK,

 110

didn't she?' said Emily. She clapped her hands and did a little dance.

'OK isn't exactly yes. Hey, that's the Prance Dance, isn't it?' I asked.

'Yes! Shall I show you how to do it?' Emily offered.

'Who showed you?'

'Well, Chloe did, when she came round on Saturday,' said Emily, doing all kinds of little prancing steps and a few wiggles too. 'Come on, copy me!'

'It looks a bit silly,' I said, not wanting to make a complete fool of myself in the playground with everyone watching.

Emily misunderstood. 'I look silly?' she said, hurt.

'No! I just meant it's a silly dance,' I said.

'Well, you might think that but Mattie Rayburn's gazillion followers think it's fantastic,' said Emily.

'All right, all right. Sorry. Don't get in a huff,' I said.

'I'm not,' said Emily. 'I'm happy happy happy because now we're both going to the Best Sleepover in the World.'

'I'm happy happy happy too,' I said, giving her a hug. 'Thank you for sticking up for me to Chloe. You're the best friend ever, Emily.'

I tried my best to *feel* happy, but it didn't work. Whenever I looked up in class that afternoon Chloe seemed to be staring at me. I hated the way her eyes gleamed. She had everyone in her power now. Especially me.

'Guess what,' I said to Mum when she came to collect me from school.

'Let me see,' said Mum. 'Chloe's having her own private spaceship to take everyone to the moon and back at her sleepover party?'

'Oh, ha ha,' I said. 'No, she's actually invited me to it now.'

'Really?' said Mum. 'Well, I hope you had a moment of total triumph saying, "No thank you – I'm going to a *much* better sleepover on Friday night!"'

I gave another little laugh, my throat drying. 'Mum, does Lily's sleepover have to be *this* Friday?'

Mum looked puzzled. 'Well, of course it does. That's the whole point. Lily's so excited!'

'Yes, I suppose so,' I said. I didn't feel able to press the point further then. I had a feeling Mum might be disappointed in me. Deep down I was disappointed in myself.

Lily was almost beside herself when Jeff brought her back from school. She was signing in such a frenzy that we couldn't understand her. She was doing her best to talk too, going, 'Ur ur ur *ur*!' and looking at Jeff.

'Hello, darling,' said Mum. 'What's happened? You're very excited!'

Lily laughed, agreeing. She pointed at Jeff again.

'What is it, Jeff?' Mum asked.

'Oh, nothing much. Well, Lily and Natalie were going on about this famous sleepover on Friday, and young Natalie said she wished they could go swimming, so Jen and I put our heads together and

 114

decided that Jen and her friend Stevie, who works at the school too, could keep the pool open Friday afternoon. The girls can have a bit of a frolic in the pool, and then after I've taken my regular kids home I'll come back and switch the boiler off and close the pool down for the holidays.'

'Oh my goodness, how kind of you!' said Mum. 'Are you certain? Surely you'll all want to hurry home on the last day of term?'

'We'd like the girls to have a bit of fun. You can come too, Daisy,' said Jeff. 'And your best friend.'

I didn't know what to say. Lily chortled with joy. Mum gave me a nudge.

'Say thank you, Daisy,' she said.

'Thank you very much,' I said helplessly. 'That would be lovely.'

Chapter Twelve

I couldn't tell Lily I'd been invited to Chloe's famous Best Sleepover in the World. Or that I wanted to go to it. I wanted to go to it desperately.

Lily was so happy she couldn't get to sleep. I couldn't either. I crept into her room in the middle of the night and she was wide awake. She wasn't fussing though. She was crooning to herself, as if she was singing a song.

I got into bed beside her and we cuddled up. Our arms were round each other, so Lily couldn't sign, but she didn't need to. I knew what she was thinking. She was thrilled she was going to have a special sleepover, especially now she could have a private swim.

I knew I couldn't let her down. I was sad I couldn't go to Chloe's party. I was terrified that Emily would go without me and be Chloe's best friend again. But I was also a little bit happy simply because Lily was happy.

I told Emily the next day.

'I can't go to Chloe's sleepover. I can't upset Lily. She's really looking forward to her own sleepover and it's all arranged now,' I said.

'Oh!' said Emily. She looked stricken.

I hesitated. I didn't want to say it but I felt I had to.

'It's OK. You can still go to Chloe's party if you want,' I said.

'Really?' said Emily.

It wasn't what I'd hoped she'd say. I suppose *I* looked stricken now.

'But I don't want to,' Emily said quickly. 'No – I'll still come to Lily's sleepover.'

'Oh, Emily!' I said. 'Will you tell Chloe?'

Emily pulled a face. 'Maybe not just yet. You know what she can be like. But I won't go to her sleepover – I promise.'

That meant so much. Emily joined all the others clustering round Chloe while she boasted that everyone was going to be given a goodie bag of Little Princess products when they had their makeover, but I knew Emily was only biding her time.

She was still biding her time on Wednesday. She promised again and again that she'd tell Chloe when the right moment arose, but it never seemed to come.

'I'll tell her first thing tomorrow, cross my heart,' said Emily when we said goodbye.

But Emily wasn't at school first thing on Thursday. She always got to school early, but not this day.

Chloe came over to me, hands on her hips. 'Where's Emily then?' she asked.

I shrugged. 'I don't know,' I mumbled.

'I thought you two were such best friends,' said Chloe, sneering.

I wanted to slap her, though of course that's not allowed. You must never hit anyone, even if she's your worst enemy. But I *wanted* to.

Mrs Graham came into the classroom and started taking the register. She called Emily's name and there was a weird little silence. She called Emily's name again and saw her chair was empty. Then she went on to the next girl on the list. She obviously didn't know why Emily wasn't there – but she'd found out by lunchtime.

She was on playground duty and found me huddled in a corner. I was trying to read a book.

But I kept going over the same page. The words wouldn't stay in my head.

'Hello, Daisy. Oh dear, you look a bit lonely sitting here all by yourself. Why don't you go and play with Amy and Bella?' said Mrs Graham.

I couldn't go and play with Amy and Bella because I wasn't sure we were still friends, and they were in the crowd round Chloe anyway. Surely Mrs Graham could work that out for herself?

Perhaps she did, because she squatted down beside me, looking concerned.

'Are you missing Emily?' she asked.

I nodded.

'I've found out what's the matter. Her mother rang the office. Poor Emily's got that stomach bug that Bethany had. Let's hope it's not going to be making its way around the class. It would be such a shame if Chloe caught it and couldn't enjoy this extraordinary sleepover of hers.' She said it sympathetically, but I thought I saw an odd twinkle in her eyes. Maybe Mrs Graham didn't like Chloe any more than I did.

'Did Chloe tell you all about her sleepover, Mrs Graham?' I asked.

'She didn't need to,' said Mrs Graham. 'The entire school is buzzing with it. Everyone wants to go to it.'

'I don't,' I muttered. 'Actually I'm going to *another* sleepover on Friday. It's my sister Lily's.'

'Oh, that's nice,' said Mrs Graham. She paused. 'And is Emily coming too, if she's better?'

'Yes,' I said. 'Yes, she promised.'

I perked up a little – but when we were going back into school Chloe caught up with me.

'You do know why Emily's not at school, don't you?' she said.

'Yes, she's got a stomach bug,' I said.

'No, she hasn't. She's just pretending. She's staying away because she doesn't dare tell you that

 123

she's not coming to your weird sister's pathetic little sleepover. She's coming to *mine*,' said Chloe.

'That's not true!' I said – but already doubts were buzzing in my head like bees. Could it be true? I told myself Chloe was only winding me up but I couldn't be certain.

When I got home I asked Mum if I could use her mobile and phone Emily. I had to talk to her mum first because Emily doesn't have her own mobile either.

'Hello, Mrs Evans, it's me, Daisy,' I said.

'Hello, Daisy,' she said. She sounded distracted. I could hear Emily's little brother howling in the background.

'Please can I talk to Emily?' I asked.

'It's not really a good time, dear,' said Emily's mum. 'She's not feeling very well.'

'Couldn't I just have a little word? I promise I won't take long,' I said.

'I can't really get her. She's upstairs in the bathroom and I'm downstairs trying to change the baby. Oh, Ben, shh, I can't hear myself think. I'm sorry, Daisy, I've got to go.'

'Can you tell Emily I rang?' I asked desperately.

'Of course,' she said vaguely, and then cut the phone off.

I stared at Mum's mobile, imagining I could still hear Emily's mum's voice. Was she calling to Emily, saying, 'Do you think you're going to be sick again, darling? I'll be up in a minute, pet, after I've changed Ben.' Or was she saying, 'Daisy sounds

rather worried about you, Emily. I think you really must stop pretending to be poorly and tell her the truth.'

Chapter Thirteen

Lily came home looking so happy again. I did my best to act cheerful but it wasn't easy. Mum was having a hard time too, worrying about the food for Lily's sleepover party.

'What would you like to eat, darling?' she asked Lily.

Lily held out one hand and curled her other over it, signing 'cake'.

'Yes, I know. Natalie wants cake. Grandad will be making you a totally splendid Black Forest gateau. That's sorted. But we can't only eat cake. What else should I give you? Does Natalie like sandwiches? I made a little picnic for Daisy's sleepover, remember?' Mum asked.

'Lily can't remember because she got upset and cried a lot and had to be put to bed,' I said.

Lily put her hand over her mouth, signing 'shut up'. She looked embarrassed.

'Yes, well, let's hope that doesn't happen this time,' said Mum quickly. 'Lily, does Natalie ever have a crying fit?'

'No!' Lily signed, with one wave of her hand. Then she stroked her fingers on the palm of her other hand. That meant 'Happy!' She signed it three times, smiling now.

'Well, that's good. And you'll both have a happy time,' said Mum, though she still looked anxious. 'So? Egg sandwiches? Cheese? Banana?'

Lily touched her first finger with all the other fingers on her other hand. This was a new one on Mum and me.

Lily signed again, more emphatically, and smacked her lips together. I'd seen her doing that many times before. I suddenly got it.

'Pasta!' I said.

'You can't have *pasta* sandwiches!' said Mum.

Lily was chortling.

'She's joking!' I said, laughing too.

'You girls!' said Mum.

She told Dad about Lily's joke when he got home from work. He smiled and tickled Lily under her chin.

'Actually, why not give them pasta?' he asked.

'I can't make it properly, that's why,' said Mum. 'I haven't got a pasta-making machine for a start.'

'You can just get the ready-made stuff from the supermarket,' said Dad. 'And packets of sauce. There you go. Easy-peasy.'

'But it doesn't taste anywhere near as nice as Mrs Morelli's pasta. That's the sort Lily likes best,' said Mum.

'Aha!' said Dad.

After we'd had supper (sausages and mash, but the sausages were a bit burnt and the mash a little lumpy – Mum really isn't all that great at cooking), Dad said he was quickly nipping out to Morelli's.

'Dad! You've only just had four sausages and a huge mound of mash!' I said. Dad is very loyal and always eats up Mum's food. He often eats Lily's and my leftovers too.

'Are you thinking of booking a meal there for tomorrow?' Mum asked. 'I don't think that would work with two big wheelchairs in that little restaurant.'

'I'm going to ask Mrs Morelli if she'd consider doing a big takeaway tomorrow. Enough for . . . how many people? Mum and me, Daisy and Emily, and Natalie. One, two, three, four, five. I haven't

left anyone out, have I?'

Lily thumped herself on the chest.

'Oh! *Lily!*' said Dad. He'd only been joking.

Lily laughed. Mum laughed too.

'Great idea!' she said.

It was a great idea – but maybe we *would* just be five people.

I didn't sleep properly that night. I stayed awake, lying on my front, my back and both sides, thinking about Emily. Perhaps she was tossing and turning too, thinking about me. I didn't get to sleep until the middle of the night. I was so tired I didn't wake up in the morning when Dad went to work and Mum started organizing Lily. Mum didn't shake me awake until it was quarter past eight.

'Wake up, sleepyhead,' she said. She'd brought me a bowl of cornflakes and a glass of orange juice.

'Gobble up your breakfast and then get washed and dressed as quickly as you can or we'll be late for school. Jeff's here for Lily. She's *so* excited!'

I listened in a daze.

'Has Emily rung?' I asked.

'No, lovie.'

'Can I phone her mum again to see if she's still sick?'

'There's no time – and she'll be busy with the baby anyway. You'll find out about Emily soon enough when you get to school. If she's still sick then maybe you'd like to ask one of your other friends to come tonight – though I suppose it's a bit late notice,' said Mum.

I wasn't sure I had any other friends now. I hoped Amy and Bella were still sort-of friends but they were going to Chloe's sleepover tonight.

'Daisy! Don't daydream, darling. Eat your cornflakes.'

I picked up my spoon and then dumped it back in the bowl. 'I don't feel hungry,' I said.

'Oh, Daisy, don't be difficult,' said Mum.

'I feel sick,' I said.

Mum took a deep breath. 'Don't say you're going down with this sickness bug,' she said. 'What am I

going to do? I can't cancel everything now. Lily
would be devastated.'

'Oh, Lily, Lily, Lily,' I said, climbing out of bed.
'I'm sick to death of everyone putting Lily first all
the time. I could be going to Chloe's sleepover if it
wasn't for Lily. You never think about me. You love
Lily way more than you love me!'

'Daisy! How can you say that? I'm ashamed of
you,' said Mum.

I was ashamed of me too, especially as I was sure
Lily had come up with the idea of having a sleepover
to comfort me. I stomped my way to the bathroom,
had the quickest of washes and then tugged on my
school uniform. Mum was in the kitchen now,
making me a slice of toast and honey.

'Here, eat this on your way to school,' she said,
folding it into a sandwich. 'And gulp down your juice.'

I gulped obediently and took a bite of toast.

'Sorry,' I mumbled, with my mouth full.

'Oh, Daisy, I'm sorry too. I know it's really hard for you at times. You're always such a loving sister to Lily that I tend to take it for granted. But surely you know I love you both absolutely equally, you silly sausage,' Mum said, giving me a big hug.

'I know,' I said, giving Mum a big hug back. I might have got a smear of honey on her T-shirt but I hoped she wouldn't mind.

We hurried to school and got to the playground just as the bell was ringing.

'You're very pale,' said Mum. 'You're not really feeling sick, are you?'

I shook my head, munching my last bite of toast.

'I do hope Emily's in school today and feeling fine,' said Mum.

 136

I hoped so too. I hoped and hoped and hoped. But she wasn't at her desk.

'Is Emily still sick, Mrs Graham?' I asked in a rush.

'Daisy, I'm Emily's teacher, not her mother,' said Mrs Graham. 'I really don't know. Now sit down at once and get out your English notebook. I want everyone to write a story with a surprise ending.'

I was usually really good at making up stories. But today I couldn't manage a proper beginning, let alone an ending. I kept starting to write a sentence, and then losing track of my thoughts, so

I had to cross the few words out and start again.
By the end of the lesson I'd only managed half a
page, and that was mostly crossings out.

Most of the class seemed to be having difficulties
too. The Chloe Gang and Amy and Bella and Sam
and Richard were all buzzing with excitement
because they were going to attend the Best Sleepover
in the World. The rest of the class were so envious
they couldn't concentrate, desperate for Chloe to
change her mind and invite them at the last minute.
Chloe herself was as pink and sparkly as the slides
in her hair.

Chapter Fourteen

Chloe came up to me at break time. Everyone followed her, gathering around.

'Still worried about Emily?' she said to me.

'She's sick,' I said.

'Can I come to your sleepover party, Chloe, instead of Emily then?' Bethany asked. She was now completely better.

'Oh, sorry, Bethany, afraid not,' said Chloe. She

was looking straight at me. 'Emily's just *pretending* to be sick to keep out of Daisy's way. She doesn't want her to know she's coming to *my* sleepover.'

'No, she's not pretending,' I said, though I was starting to believe it now.

'Emily is a *little* bit sick though,' said Chloe. 'Sick of being Daisy's friend. She wants to break up with her and go back to being *my* friend. Doesn't she, Bella? Doesn't she, Amy?'

Bella and Amy looked uncomfortable. They looked at me. They looked at Chloe.

'I don't know about that,' Bella mumbled.

'Emily hasn't said anything to us,' said Amy, biting her nail anxiously.

'Well, you'll find out when you see her at my sleepover party tonight,' said Chloe. She paused. '*If* you're still coming?'

Chloe was making it plain they had to gang up against me or they wouldn't be able to come.

'Still, never mind. You can go to Daisy's pathetic sleepover instead and play with her dumb zombie sister.' Chloe pulled a terrible face, pretending to be Lily.

'How dare you!' I cried, trembling all over. 'Lily isn't dumb – that's a horrid word. She uses sign language instead of speaking language. And she's not a zombie either; she's kind and funny and I'll tell you what – she doesn't ever wet herself!' This wasn't strictly true, but I didn't care.

Chloe gave a little gasp. She went very red. She stared at me, her eyes wide. She was silently pleading,

scared I'd tell everyone what had happened.

I wanted to tell the entire school. I wanted to tell the whole street, the whole town, the whole world, so that everyone would point their finger and laugh at Chloe and she'd never have power over anyone again.

I'd have the power.

Chapter Fifteen

I wasn't sure I wanted to be a Chloe. I wanted people to be friends with me because they *liked* me. *I* wanted to like me. So I clamped my mouth shut to stop all the fierce, spiteful things I wanted to say. Everyone was looking at me, waiting. Amy and Bella were obviously wondering when I was going to come right out with it.

The silence seemed to have been going on for six

hours at least but I suppose it was only six seconds. I swallowed hard, and then I heard someone whisper, 'What's she going on about? *Who* wet herself?'

I managed to say, 'Oh, no one. I was just sticking up for my sister.' I watched Chloe. 'Don't you dare say anything mean about my sister ever again,' I hissed at her.

Chloe didn't reply but she gave the slightest little nod. Then I walked away. I was still trembling. I had to keep blinking because my eyes were blurry. But somehow I felt OK.

I heard footsteps behind me. Was it Chloe running to say she was sorry and she'd never be mean to me again? Of course not! It was Amy and Bella.

'Are you all right, Daisy? You're not crying, are you? Chloe was dreadful to say those nasty things,' said Amy.

'I wish I hadn't said I'd go to her sleepover now,' said Bella. 'Who cares about swimming in that Blue Door pool?'

'And so what if Mattie Rayburn is going to be at Chloe's?' said Amy. 'I can watch her any old time on my sister's phone.'

'It's OK, really,' I said. 'Just as long as we're still friends.'

'Of course we are,' said Bella, offering me a square of her chocolate.

'You bet,' said Amy. 'And take no notice of Chloe. I don't think Emily's going to her sleepover. She's your best friend for ever.'

'Absolutely,' said Bella.

* * *

AND THEY WERE RIGHT!!!

When the bell rang for us to go back into school, Emily was in the class, sitting at her desk! I rubbed my eyes, thinking I must be imagining her. But no, there she was, totally real. She got up and threw her arms round me.

'You're back!' I said joyfully. I lowered my voice. 'Were you only pretending to be sick?'

'No, I was, truly. Mum thought I had this sickness bug and said I had to stay off school. I felt heaps better this morning, so when I wasn't sick after

 146

breakfast she let me come to school. She doesn't think it's a bug after all, just my nervous stomach,' said Emily.

Amy and Bella and I peered at her tummy with interest but it looked quite ordinary under her school uniform. But then our own stomachs felt nervous when we saw Chloe approaching.

'So you're better,' she said. 'Just in time to come to my sleepover party.'

'It sounds as if it will be a lovely party,' said Emily. 'Thank you very much for asking me – but I'm going to Lily's sleepover.'

She said it calmly, but I could see her hands clasped tight under her desk. Chloe didn't argue. She knew when she was beaten. She shrugged and spat out one word: 'Loser!' Then she marched off.

'You're a *winner*, Emily,' I said.

'I kept rehearsing what I was going to say inside my head until I knew it off by heart,' said Emily.

'Shall I say I can't come to her sleepover too?' said Amy.

'I should say it too. I was the one who started all this,' said Bella. 'I wish I'd kept my big mouth shut now.'

I stared across at Chloe. She was giving out little midnight-blue cards sprinkled with glitter, with instructions on how to get to the Blue Door club. She was busy telling everyone the time they had to get there after school, showing off like anything – but her voice was high-pitched

and her shoulders were drooping. I found myself feeling weirdly sorry for her.

'You two go and get your invitation cards,' I said to Amy and Bella. 'I don't mind a bit.'

'Yes, we'll want you to go so we can hear all about it,' said Emily.

So they went off to Chloe – and Emily gave my hand a squeeze.

'I'd much much rather be at Lily's sleepover with you,' she said.

Chapter Sixteen

It was lovely of Emily to be so kind but I was still worried. We really weren't going to do very much at Lily's sleepover. We were just going to have a splash with Lily and her friend Natalie in a small water-therapy pool. Then we were having supper at my home and hopefully Uncle Gary would pop in to see us. After that we'd hang out together for a bit. And then go to bed.

It didn't sound very exciting. And it might be a bit awkward. Would we be able to think of things to say to each other? Emily didn't know Makaton so she might feel a bit left out. I seemed to be developing a nervous stomach too because it wouldn't stop churning.

We played games in class all afternoon because it was our last day at school. Mrs Graham divided us into little teams and we played charades. I organized our charade. Emily and Amy and Bella and I put our hands together on one side of our faces and closed our eyes. Then we jiggled our arms up and down. We thought it was easy-peasy but no one guessed for ages.

Mrs Graham laughed. 'I would have thought you would have guessed straight away, Chloe, seeing as you've talked of nothing else for days,' she said.

'Anyway, I hope you all have a lovely time and enjoy yourselves whether you're going to the Best Sleepover in the World or not.'

'Are you *sure* you don't want to go to Chloe's sleepover instead?' I asked Emily. 'I'm sure Chloe would let you still come.'

'For goodness' sake!' said Emily. She knocked

gently on my head. 'Hello? Is there a girl called Daisy inside? Could you tell her I'm definitely coming to her sister's sleepover? It's all arranged. Come on!'

We dashed out of the cloakroom as Chloe was dashing in, followed by a gang of girls still asking endless questions about when and where they were meeting. Sam and Richard were in hot pursuit. In fact, Richard tried to scurry right into the girls' toilets until Sam yanked him out again.

Chloe and I had to dodge round each other. She looked at me. I looked at her.

'Have a great time, Chloe,' I said. I'm not sure I meant it, but it seemed the right thing to say, seeing as she'd lost the battle over Emily.

She looked taken aback. Then she took a deep breath. I wondered what mean thing she was going

to say. Maybe she was even going to spit at me. She didn't. She just nodded. She didn't manage to say, 'You have a great time too.' But that sort of made me the winner, not the loser.

My mum and Emily's mum were standing together behind the playground railings. Emily and I went dashing over to them. Emily's mum had baby Ben on her hip. He chuckled when he saw Emily and went, 'Em Em Em!'

'He can talk already!' I said.

'Well, not really. He calls everyone Em Em Em,' said Emily.

'I wonder if he can speak Makaton?' I said. 'Hello!' I waved my hand once. 'Go "hello", Ben. Hello! Hello!' I signed.

Ben blinked at me solemnly as if he thought I was a very silly person, but then he raised his

arm and waved a perfect 'hello' sign!

'That's amazing!' said Emily's mum, laughing.

Ben laughed too, very pleased with himself.

'Teach him some more, Daisy,' Emily begged.

'Lily should teach him,' I said. 'She taught me.'

An enormous gleaming limousine drew up right outside the school gates, exactly where you're not allowed to park. A very tanned man with a bald head, a fancy shirt and a huge gold watch tooted his horn and waved, and Chloe came flying across the playground.

'Dad, Dad, Dad!' she cried.

'Hello, Princess. Your carriage awaits,' he called, blowing her kisses.

Emily and I rolled our eyes. Our mums raised their eyebrows. Chloe's dad waved at Emily's mum.

'See you and young Emily at the Blue Door club at five,' he called.

'Sorry, Rich, Emily's not coming,' Emily's mum called.

'But Chloe said she was. Definitely,' said Chloe's dad.

'No, I don't *want* her to come, Daddy,' said Chloe in a silly baby voice.

'Whoops! Have I put my foot in it again?' said Chloe's dad, pulling a silly face. 'In you get, little sweetheart.'

Chloe climbed in the back, ignoring all the Girl Gang and Sam and Richard. They went on

waving and calling until the limousine turned the corner.

'Is he called Rich because he *is* rich?' I asked.

'He's Richard,' said Emily's mum. Then she turned to Mum. She lowered her voice, but I've got sharp ears. 'Thank goodness Emily is best friends with your Daisy now!'

Emily heard too, and we nudged each other.

Then Emily's mum handed over her bag containing her swimming things, her favourite dress, her pyjamas, her toothbrush and teddy, and hugged her goodbye. Ben tugged Emily's hair, but not too hard. I showed him how to sign 'goodbye', and his mum made his chubby little hand wave away.

Then Mum and Emily and I walked up the road to where Mum had parked our car. We usually walked home but we were going to Lily's school which is miles away. I felt a bit embarrassed when Emily saw our car.

'It's a mobility car. It has to be big enough for Lily's wheelchair,' I explained. 'That's why it looks a bit weird.'

'I think it looks great,' said Emily valiantly. 'It's good there's lots of room for Lily at the back.'

'Will we be able to squeeze Natalie's wheelchair

in too, Mum?' I asked.

'Natalie's mother says she can manage without one. She walks with a frame,' said Mum.

'Will Lily be able to walk one day?' I asked.

'Probably not,' said Mum.

'That's not fair,' I said. I felt so sorry for Lily. I'd hate it if my friend could walk and talk and I couldn't.

'Still, perhaps she'll be able to use her wheel-chair independently when she's older,' said Mum.

'And if not I can always push her around. She likes it when I push her now, doesn't she,' I said proudly.

I was very keen to see what Lily's school was really like.

Our school's quite old and it only has a climbing frame and two football nets in the playground.

Lily's school seemed very new. It had a large garden with smooth, wide paths dividing it into big squares, so that children could move round easily in their wheelchairs. There was a big play area with a special soft surface, big nets for different kinds of games, a slide with built-up sides, and a sandpit for the younger ones.

'No wonder Lily likes it at her school,' I said.

We went into the entrance where a cosy-looking receptionist was whistling as she packed up her shoulder bag.

'It's the holidays, hurray!' she said. 'You must be here for Lily's party. You'll find her in the swimming pool with Natalie. Have fun!'

The pool didn't have midnight-blue tiles or stars twinkling on the ceiling. It was just a small heated pool with special hoists and wide steps – but there

was a lovely seaside mural on one wall and a flock of papier mâché seagulls bobbed up and down on strings above us.

Jen and her friend Stevie were already in the pool in their swimming costumes, supporting Lily and Natalie. Jen was exactly as I'd imagined: smiley, her hair tied back in a ponytail, wearing a red costume with *The Boss!* in white lettering on the front. Stevie was small and wiry, but her skinny arms still looked very muscly. She had very short hair with a little quiff.

Of course I knew what Lily looked like, though it was a lovely surprise to see her bobbing about out of her wheelchair, with Jen's strong arms supporting her. Natalie was the biggest surprise of all. She was

a bit older than Lily. She had very long, straight, jet-black hair that trailed behind her in the turquoise water. She was very pale, almost ghostly white, and wore a black swimming costume. She had black eyeliner painted round her eyes and black nail polish, even on her toenails. She had black spiders on her arms. I thought they were tattoos but I think they were only inked on because they started to smudge in the water.

Natalie was a goth!

Chapter Seventeen

'Hello!' said Natalie. She signed with a wave of her hand but she spoke too. Her voice was very low and strange, but I could understand it. 'I'm Nat.'

Lily signed 'hello' too and was so pleased to see us she thumped the water. She splashed Jen by accident, but Jen just laughed. Lily concentrated hard, managed to get both hands curved in front of her and made them bob up and down. Then she put

her hands together by her face and *then* made her hands jiggle about. Jen had to hang on hard to her or she might have capsized in her efforts.

'She's saying welcome to her sleepover party!' I said.

'How do I say thank you?' Emily asked.

Lily and Natalie both touched their chins and then brought their hand away.

'Thank you!' said Natalie.

'Thank *you*!' Emily and I both said together.

'And a very big thank you to Jen and Stevie for letting you girls have this special treat,' said Mum, smiling happily. 'Hello, Lily darling. Hello, Natalie. I'm Lily's mum and this is Daisy and her best friend Emily,' said Mum.

Lily pointed to Natalie and they both touched their own thumbs and then clasped their hands,

signing that they were best friends too.

'Lily's my best friend now and I'm hers,' said Natalie. She looked at Jen. 'Jen thinks I am a bad influence but she's only joking.'

Lily signed she was very good, with both her thumbs up. Natalie gave a great grin and signed with her two little fingers in the air, which means 'very naughty'.

No wonder Lily was proud to have Natalie as a best friend. Natalie was so cool. Emily was a little bit shy of her at first, and got a bit muddled by the signing, but once we were in the pool we all had lots of fun together.

I usually hate the getting-in part because the water always feels very cold and it takes me ages to get my shoulders under, but this pool was like climbing into the loveliest warm bath. It wasn't

really deep so you didn't have that scary feeling when you tried to put your feet down for a rest and found you couldn't touch the bottom. The water wasn't midnight blue but it was a perfect pool otherwise.

Lily and Natalie usually did therapy exercises in the pool, with just five minutes play at the end of the session, but as it was Lily's party we could play the whole time. Lily and Natalie couldn't swim by themselves, but Jen and Stevie could tow them along really quickly. I was quite a good swimmer but I mostly came last when we had races. Emily generally came first, though Jen was very fast and Stevie beat Emily twice.

'Let's duck them,' Natalie said to me, but she was only joking.

We had proper party games too, playing Piggy-

in-the-Middle with balloons, and then we had rides on great big inflatables. They were the best. I had a blue dolphin, Emily had a pink one, Lily had a giant orange goldfish and Natalie had a shark with big painted teeth. Emily and I made little dolphin squeaks, Lily opened and shut her mouth like a goldfish, and Natalie tried hard to look menacing, showing her teeth.

We were having so much fun we wanted to stay in the pool for ages, but eventually Mum said we must really let Jen and Stevie go home. She gave them a giant box of chocolates for being so kind. They said they'd had fun too. Jen opened the box then and there and let us all choose one when we'd got out of the pool. Emily and I took turns using one of the sit-down showers, washing each other's hair,

playing as though we had our own salon. We actually took longer to get changed than Lily and Natalie, and they had to have a lot of help.

Emily put on her favourite dress, blue with a pattern of little white kittens. I got dressed in my own favourite, which is bright red with sprigs of yellow flowers. It's got matching knickers too, though I hope they don't show. Mum had brought Lily's favourite outfit too. It's a pink smock dress with a very flouncy skirt. It's not very practical when you have to use a wheelchair, but Mum understood that Lily needed to feel pretty above all else.

When Jen wheeled Lily out of her changing room I put my fingers to my lips and then splayed them out, signing 'beautiful'. Emily copied me. Lily looked enormously pleased.

Natalie couldn't have dressed more differently to

Lily. She wore a black T-shirt with a screaming ghost on it, black jeans and black boots with complicated buckles. She'd made her own black bead bracelets and wore a black leather string with a black pendant on it. Stevie must have been very patient helping with so many buckles and beads, but she'd done her best.

'Ta dah!' said Natalie as she emerged from the curtains. She had a special frame so she could push herself along, though she had to go slowly and her legs wobbled a lot.

Lily bent her hand downwards and waggled her fingers as best she could. I wasn't sure what this twiddly bit meant.

'Spider girl!' said Natalie, laughing. 'Yay! Call me Tarantula!' She had to repeat it several times before we understood, and then we laughed with her.

It took quite a lot of organizing getting Natalie and Lily and Emily and me all into the car, but Mum managed it, strapping Natalie into the front seat. Emily and I squashed up together in the back, with Lily in her wheelchair like a queen on her throne.

When we got home Dad was back from work early, waiting at the front door for us. He pretended to be frightened of Natalie in her goth outfit, which pleased her enormously. He ushered us into the living room. He'd decorated it with balloons and the Christmas fairy lights and arranged Lily's and my teddies and dolls on a pillow with a shawl over them so it looked as if they were having a sleepover too.

'We don't actually play with them nowadays,' I said hurriedly. 'It's just Dad mucking about.'

We were all starving hungry after our swimming

session so it was good to see the table set with the best plates and knives and forks. There was even a big vase of white flowers in the middle of the table – lilies!

'I love lilies,' said Natalie, crossing her hands over her chest to sign 'love'. 'People put them on *graves*.'

Emily looked at me anxiously.

'It's OK. I think she's only joking, isn't she?' I said.

Lily nodded her fist and then stroked her chin with her thumb and first finger. I knew what that meant: 'laugh!'

Mum brought in a jug of elderflower cordial for us. She'd

tactfully put three glasses and two beakers on the tray because she wasn't quite sure which Natalie would use. She chose a glass, but her hands were a bit shaky and she spilled some down her front. It didn't matter because her T-shirt was mostly black.

Dad said he was just popping down the road.

'Is he going for a drink?' Emily whispered to me. 'That's what my dad does when it's his turn to bath Ben and put him to bed.'

'No, he's only going to fetch supper,' I said.

'Oh, good! Is it fish and chips?' Natalie asked.

Lily concentrated hard and managed to put the fingers and thumbs of her left hand touching the first finger of her right hand.

'What does that mean?' said Emily.

'Pasta!' said Natalie enthusiastically.

'And then cake, Natalie,' I said.

'I love cake!' said Natalie.

'I think you'll especially love this cake,' I said. 'It's black.'

'What, like chocolate?' Natalie asked.

'There's lots of chocolate and chocolate cream and cherries too, isn't that right, Lily?' I said.

She made both of her hands nod.

Dad came back from Morelli's with special bags clutched to his chest. Mrs Morelli had sent an enormous vat of her special cheesy pasta, enough for twelve people, not six, so we could all have double portions. She sent breadsticks too, and a big tomato salad and zucchini fritters, so we had a positive feast.

I wondered if Lily would feel embarrassed because she wasn't any good at handling cutlery and she felt such a baby when Mum fed her – but Natalie

sat close to Lily's wheelchair and fed her a mouthful at a time, and helped her drink too.

'We eat together in the canteen, don't we, Lily,' she said. 'Because we're best friends.'

'Daisy and I are best friends too,' said Emily, and I smiled at her fondly.

When we'd eaten our fill we had a little rest and then Mum brought in Grandad's Black Forest gateau.

'Wow!' said Natalie and Emily simultaneously.

I looked across at Lily and winked at her.

'Did you make it?' Natalie asked Mum.

Lily signed no and then tackled a sign that involved clenching one fist and tapping two fingers on top of it.

'Grandad?' said Natalie. 'Wow!'

This Black Forest gateau was even better than the first.

'How do you sign "absolutely yummy"?' Emily asked, and Lily and Natalie signed with a thumb across their upper lip. Emily and I copied.

Then there was a knock at the door.

'I think it's Uncle Gary!' I said, running to answer first.

I was right and wrong all at the same time!

Chapter Eighteen

I stared at the overwhelmingly glorious person standing on the doorstep. She had fair wavy hair past her shoulders, with a huge diamanté clip tucking back some of her blonde locks to show off one ear decorated with a matching diamanté earring. She wore a red satin tightly fitting dress, little black gloves and immensely high black shoes with heels that looked dagger-sharp.

She smiled at me, her long false eyelashes fluttering, her ruby lips forming a perfect Cupid's bow. I was utterly overcome. I wondered who on earth she was – a film actress, a television star, a famous singer?

'Hello, darling Princess Daisy!' she said, blowing me a kiss from her glossy lips. There was something very familiar about her voice, her sparkly blue eyes, her sweet smile.

'Oh my goodness! You're not – you can't be – are you *Uncle Gary*?'

'I am indeed, sweetheart, though I'm in my work clothes tonight, so you'd better call me Gloriette, my professional name,' she said. 'Is it

OK for me to come in? I don't want to give Lily too much of a shock.'

'She'll be thrilled!' I said. 'Bend down, Gloriette, so I can give you a big kiss.'

'Oh, you darling child!' said Gloriette. 'Try not to lick my blusher off though!'

I burst out laughing, took hold of her hand, and pulled her inside.

Mum and Dad were in the hall.

'Gary, what are you *like*?' said Mum. 'You didn't say you'd come dressed for your act!'

'I egged him on,' said Dad. 'Gary, mate, you look *amazing*!'

'Thank you, darling. All compliments gratefully accepted,' said Gloriette, in a surprisingly girly voice.

I took her hand and pulled her into the living

room. Lily and Natalie and Emily looked at her in amazement.

'It's OK, Lily, it's only—' I started, but Lily got it before I could finish. She put two fingers one side of her chin and then the other side. I knew that sign! It was Makaton for 'uncle'. She absolutely squealed with laughter.

'Wow!' said Natalie. 'You look awesome!'

'So do you,' said Gloriette. 'You must be Natalie, Lily's best friend. And *you* must be Emily, Daisy's best friend.'

Emily was looking a bit anxious.

'Don't worry, Emily, it's just my Uncle Gary dressed up as a lady,' I whispered.

'I *am* a lady, you saucebox,' said Gloriette, tapping me on the nose. Then she turned to Lily. 'Hello, my party princess.' She swept her the most

magnificent curtsy, which was quite difficult in the tight dress and high heels.

Lily laughed and laughed. 'Cake, Uncle?' she signed.

'It's fantastic cake!' said Natalie. 'I'll have another slice!'

'Ah, I see Grandad's done you proud, Lily,' said Gloriette, looking at the glorious Black Forest

gateau. 'I'd love a slice, but I have to think of my figure, girl.'

Lily held her hands out and then moved them much closer together.

'Is that the sign for 'small'?' Emily asked and was thrilled to see she'd got it right.

Gloriette helped all of us to another small slice. She ate hers in very cautious nibbles so as not to smudge her lipstick.

'Do you really go out to work at your club dressed as Gloriette?' I asked her.

'Yes, darling, and you should see the glances I get on the bus,' she said. 'No, I drive in my car, silly!'

'So what exactly do you do there?' Natalie asked.

'I chat to the audience first. I shall tell them about my two flowery princess nieces and their dear

little friend Emily and their ultra-cool goth friend Natalie,' she said.

'Really?' Natalie asked, looking thrilled.

'And then I'll sing a song or two – well, lip sync to a streamed song. You don't want to hear my real voice! Then I'll tell a few jokes and finish with a dance. Which reminds me. I've heard a certain Miss Mattie Rayburn is in town demonstrating her Prance Dance. Want to see *my* version?'

Of course we did. Gloriette took her mobile out of her diamanté clutch bag, fiddled with it to find the right music, kicked off her high heels, lifted her tight skirt to her knees, and then pressed the screen. A silly little song started playing, the lyrics mostly just 'Prance Dance! Prance Dance!' Gloriette leaped about, lifting her knees up high, prancing like a pony. We all collapsed with laughter.

Mum and Dad came running into the room.

'For heaven's sake, Gary, behave yourself!' said Mum.

'Go, Gary, go!' said Dad. 'In fact, *I'll* have a go!'

Dad looked even funnier, staggering around, whereas Gloriette danced beautifully, though she looked hilarious doing jazz hands, her one earring swinging as she nodded her head from side to side.

'Come on, Daisy, let's join in,' said Emily.

'I can't! I don't know the steps. I'm hopeless at dancing,' I protested.

'So's your dad!' Emily whispered.

'I heard that!' Dad puffed.

Emily went scarlet, though she could tell Dad didn't really mind.

'Lily and I will dance,' said Natalie.

She hauled herself up, ignored her walking frame

and grasped the handles of Lily's wheelchair. She wasn't strong or steady enough to push it properly, but she managed to jerk it about a bit. Lily waggled her arms more or less in time to the music, grinning.

'OK then,' I said, and stood up to dance beside Emily. I felt a total banana for the first few seconds, stumbling about, but then I picked up the beat and started prancing properly.

I pranced – we all pranced, even Mum. Actually, she was as good as Gloriette, and we all clapped her.

'This has been such *fun*!' said Emily, when we eventually flopped down, exhausted.

The fun wasn't over. Gloriette took her make-up bag out of her purse. 'A lady's make-up always has to be immaculate,' she said, patting powder on her face. 'Here, Daisy, hold the compact for me while I

touch up my eyeliner.' She applied it carefully, pulling a funny face as she did so.

'How do you get your eyeliner to flick up at the end like that?' Natalie asked. 'Mine always goes wonky.'

'It's a little trick, darling,' said Gloriette, demonstrating expertly. Then she looked at her watch. 'I've still got bags of time. Why don't I give you girls a make-up session?'

'Gary, they're far too young!' Mum protested.

'It's just for fun,' said Gloriette. 'Go on, sis. Please, Dancing Queen?'

Mum relented. Uncle Gary always knew how to get round everyone. Gloriette fetched a clean tea towel and tucked it round Lily's neck.

'You don't mind if Lily's first, do you?' Gloriette asked Natalie and Emily and me.

'Sure. It's her party,' said Natalie, smoothing Lily's long hair back gently.

We all watched as Gloriette got to work on Lily's face.

'Not too much. Not exaggerated like your make-up, Gary,' Mum insisted.

'Have faith in Gloriette, dear,' she said.

She smoothed foundation onto Lily's soft skin, dabbed pink blusher on her pale cheeks, brushed mascara on her long eyelashes and applied peachy lipstick to her mouth.

'Wow!' said Natalie, arranging Lily's hair carefully over her shoulders. 'You look stunning!'

'Oh, Lily, you look beautiful!' I said in awe.

Mum looked as if she might cry. Dad pulled out his phone to take photos of Lily.

'Do you think he – she – might make me up too?' Emily muttered.

'He/she would be delighted to do exactly that!' said Gloriette. 'Shall we be a little bit daring? How about purple eyeshadow and a beauty spot and deep crimson lips? Or orange foundation with green shadow and tiger stripes?'

'I know you're teasing me,' said Emily. 'I'd like to look pretty like Lily, please.'

'Certainly, sweetie,' said Gloriette.

Emily looked pretty without any make-up at all, but she looked positively beautiful after she'd had

her Gloriette makeover. Dad took more photos and promised to send them to Emily's mum.

'What will she *think*?' Mum fussed.

'She'll think I look lovely,' said Emily. She didn't need blusher because she was so flushed with excitement.

'Can I look lovely too, Mum, *please*?' I begged.

Mum pulled a face. 'You're such a bad influence, Gary,' she said – but she gave in!

I hardly breathed the whole time Gloriette smoothed foundation on my face and worked on my eyes and dabbed lipstick on my mouth. Then she held a mirror to my face. I'd madly hoped my features would be different and I'd look like an influencer. No, I still looked like me, with a round face and a turned-up nose and freckles – but maybe a *little* bit prettier.

I tried to do a proper pose for Dad's mobile, sucking in my cheeks and pouting, but he told me to just look natural.

'Are you ready to look natural, Natalie?' asked Gloriette.

'No way!' said Natalie in horror.

'So how about I give you those little flicks with my eyeliner and see how you look with jet black lipstick?' Gloriette suggested.

'Now you're talking!' said Natalie, seizing the tea towel from me and easing herself onto the chair.

Gloriette tactfully wiped away Natalie's smudged eyeliner and reapplied it expertly with little flicks upwards at the ends. He gave her a chalk-white foundation that covered up her few spots and then applied the promised black lipstick. Natalie's teeth flashed white as she smiled.

'Wicked!' she said.

'What about you, sis?' Gloriette offered.

'No thanks!' said Mum.

'I'll have a go!' said Dad, but Gloriette flicked her tea towel at him.

'I can't work miracles, darling!' she said. She looked at her watch again. 'Oh dear, I've really got to scoot now. I'll have to drive like the clappers to be in time for my turn at the club. Enjoy yourselves, little sweethearts,' she said, giving Mum a pot of make-up remover. 'Here, sis, this should scrape it off when they get ready for bed.'

Gloriette blew us all kisses. Lily pointed to herself, crossed her hands over her chest and then pointed to Gloriette,

signing, 'I love you'. I ran after Gloriette to the front door to give her a goodbye kiss.

'Careful, darling, we'll both smudge our make-up,' she said, but she hugged me back hard.

'Do you think Lily enjoyed meeting Gloriette?' Uncle Gary whispered in his own voice.

'She loved her, Uncle Gary! And so did I,' I said.

'I hope Emily and the little goth weren't too surprised?' he wondered.

'I bet they wish *they* had an Uncle Gary,' I said. 'Lily and I are so lucky!'

'Oh, darling, I'd do anything to please my girls,' he said.

Then he jumped in his car and drove off, waving one black-gloved hand out of the window.

Chapter Nineteen

It took ages to get our make-up off when we went to bed. We used up almost all Mum's tissues. Well, three of us did. Natalie loved her special goth make-up so much she begged and pleaded to keep it on.

'But it's so bad for your skin,' Mum protested.

'My skin's bad already,' Natalie argued.

'And it will make terrible marks on the pillow,' said Mum.

'We could cover the pillow with the tea towel,' Natalie persisted. 'Please, please, please!'

'Let her keep her make-up on if she wants to,' said Dad.

So Natalie went to bed looking triumphantly gothic. We were all in Lily's room to make it a proper sleepover with no one left out. Lily has such a big bed she could share it with Natalie. It felt a bit weird because I'm the only one who's ever shared Lily's bed up till now, but I had Emily to snuggle up with this time. Mum and Dad squeezed my mattress and bedclothes into Lily's room, and it was just as comfortable as lying in my actual bed.

Of course we didn't go to sleep straight away. You don't *sleep* at a sleepover. We kept the light on so that Lily could talk too. We watched a film for a while on Lily's computer. Natalie wanted to see a

really scary film about zombies but Lily signed 'no' very firmly. We watched an old movie about two dogs and a cat instead. Then we had a long discussion about whether we'd like a dog or a cat.

'I'm not allowed a dog because Mum says she's got her hands full already with my baby brother,' said Emily. 'I'd swap Ben for a little puppy any day of the week.'

'I wouldn't ever swap my sister but I'd like one of those poo dogs,' I said.

'All dogs poo!' said Natalie, which made us giggle.

'I meant those cuddly ones like teddy bears, a cavapoo or a cockapoo,' I said.

'They're too fluffy,' said Natalie. 'I'd like a rottweiler. Then it could scare anyone who teases me. Wouldn't you like one too, Lily?'

Lily put her fingers together and signed 'no' fiercely. Then she thought hard and signed with two fingers up either side of her chin.

'That's "cat"' said Emily. 'You've just done its whiskers!'

Lily stroked the air as if she had an imaginary cat sitting on her lap.

'Well, I'll have to keep my rottweiler at home when I next come to visit, or it will eat your cat,' said Natalie. 'I can come again, can't I, Lily? Because we're best friends, aren't we?'

Lily put both her thumbs up.

'And we're best friends,' said Emily to me. 'Do you know what? *This* has been the best sleepover in the world!'

Chapter Twenty

Amy and Bella told us all about Chloe's sleepover when we got together in the summer holidays.

'The swimming pool was magic,' said Bella. 'But Chloe sulked when we had races and I kept beating her.'

'We had Little Princess makeovers, but everyone had the same make-up. We weren't allowed to choose,' said Amy. 'And we only got a tiny lipstick

and a little mirror in our goodie bags.'

'We had an awesome tea, but the cake was all fancy icing on vanilla sponge, which was very pretty but not as good as chocolate cake,' said Bella.

'We did get to meet Mattie Rayburn. It was a meet and greet, though she just said hi to each of us. We couldn't actually *talk* to her,' said Amy. 'She did the Prance Dance but we weren't allowed to join in

the filming. They only wanted the two best dancers. Chloe got picked, of course.'

'Yet Amy's way better at dancing than Chloe,' said Bella. 'And they picked Richard too. He was so thrilled. I don't think Chloe was pleased, because he was much better than her.'

'Poor Chloe,' I said.

And I almost meant it.

ALL ABOUT MAKATON

Makaton is a special language programme that combines speech, **signs** and **symbols** to help people communicate. Signs help people who do not use speech, and symbols help people who cannot sign. It is the main programme in the UK for adults and children with communication difficulties. Makaton helps people develop communication skills such as listening to and organizing language, as well as allowing everyone to express themselves and connect with others.

Today over a hundred thousand people in the UK use Makaton to communicate, and it has been adapted in over forty countries, including Japan, South Africa and France.

Here, Lily is signing 'laugh': first make a fist and then nod it, then stroke your chin with your thumb and first finger.

To learn more, you can visit www.makaton.org and access their wide range of free resources.

DAISY AND LILY'S ULTIMATE SLEEPOVER GUIDE

Daisy and Lily are sleepover experts. Here are their tips for having the best sleepover in the world!

1. Get permission to host

Before you start planning, talk to the adults in your house about your idea and decide a date for the sleepover. It's more fun if everyone understands the rules.

2. Invite your best friends

All good sleepovers need a good invitation, and you need to make sure all your best friends are coming. Sit down, make a list – don't forget anyone! – and write the invitations. You can make them as simple

or as decorated as you like. You'll need some card, colourful pens, maybe even some glitter, and then you can add all the details.

3. Get the house ready

The invites have gone out, everyone has said yes, and now the day has come! You've got to get the house prepared before everyone arrives – if you've got a theme, you can completely transform your living room or bedroom to match it. If anyone has any accessibility needs, make sure you think about those too.

Next, you've got to make sure you've got all the right snacks. Chocolate, popcorn, cookies – the sweeter, the better!

And finally, you need to make sure that you've got enough blankets and pillows

so that everyone's warm and comfy for the evening ahead.

4. Plan some activities

No sleepover is complete without some fun activities. The possibilities here are endless: you and your friends can make your own pizzas, learn and film some dance routines, give each other makeovers, and so much more!

What would you like to do?

5. Choose the right movies

Time to settle down for the night, and a movie marathon is the perfect way to bring a sleepover to an end. What are you going to watch? Don't forget the popcorn!

YOUR TYPE OF SLEEPOVER

Take this fun quiz to find out what sort of sleepover might suit you best.

1. You overhear a classmate saying something rude about your friend. What do you do?
   - **a.** Tell your friend.
   - **b.** Tell a teacher.
   - **c.** Confront them.

2. How many friends will you invite to your sleepover?
   - **a.** Just the close ones.
   - **b.** One or two.
   - **c.** ALL OF THEM!

3. You have some free time after school and have permission to do something before going home. What do you do?

    a. Stop at the library to choose a great new book.

    b. Go and have fun at the park.

    c. Visit a friend's house.

4. How would your friends describe you?

    a. Thoughtful.

    b. Intelligent.

    c. Fun!

5. Which animal would you like to have as a pet?

    a. Cat.

    b. Rabbit.

    c. Dog.

6. What food would you like most at a sleepover?

    a. Just snacks!

    b. Pizza!

    c. Cake!

If you got mostly As

You're having a movie night! You didn't want anything too big or flashy for your sleepover, just some chill time with your friends. You can be quiet but you're loud around your friends and those you care about. Hanging out and laughing at films is your perfect night in.

If you got mostly Bs

You're going camping in the garden! You enjoy being outside and thinking things through. Camping in the garden will be a unique experience that you and your friends can all share together.

And most importantly, this means TOASTED MARSHMALLOWS!

If you got mostly Cs

It's bouncy castle time! You are super passionate about things that you love and put 110% into everything. You just want to have the best time enjoying yourself with all of your friends and the bouncy castle is the perfect way to have fun.

ALL ABOUT DAISY, LILY AND FRIENDS

Daisy

- Hates fighting with her friends
- Loves her bright red dress with yellow flowers
- Lily's little sister

Lily

- Really loves cake
- A Makaton expert!
- Daisy's big sister

Emily

- Caring and thoughtful
- Loves to play football
- Daisy's BFF

Amy

- The best dancer in class
- Has her own special way of saying hello
- Bella's BFF

Bella

- An amazing swimmer
- Obsessed with chocolate
- Amy's BFF

Have you read them all?

LAUGH OUT LOUD
THE STORY OF TRACY BEAKER
I DARE YOU, TRACY BEAKER
STARRING TRACY BEAKER
MY MUM TRACY BEAKER
WE ARE THE BEAKER GIRLS
THE WORST THING ABOUT MY
SISTER
DOUBLE ACT
FOUR CHILDREN AND IT
THE BED AND BREAKFAST STAR

HISTORICAL HEROES
HETTY FEATHER
HETTY FEATHER'S CHRISTMAS
SAPPHIRE BATTERSEA
EMERALD STAR
DIAMOND
LITTLE STARS
CLOVER MOON
ROSE RIVERS
WAVE ME GOODBYE
OPAL PLUMSTEAD
QUEENIE
DANCING THE CHARLESTON
THE RUNAWAY GIRLS
THE OTHER EDIE TRIMMER

LIFE LESSONS
THE BUTTERFLY CLUB
THE SUITCASE KID
KATY
BAD GIRLS
LITTLE DARLINGS
CLEAN BREAK
RENT A BRIDESMAID
CANDYFLOSS

THE LOTTIE PROJECT
THE LONGEST WHALE SONG
COOKIE
JACKY DAYDREAM
PAWS & WHISKERS

FAMILY DRAMAS
THE ILLUSTRATED MUM
MY SISTER JODIE
DIAMOND GIRLS
DUSTBIN BABY
VICKY ANGEL
SECRETS
MIDNIGHT
LOLA ROSE
LILY ALONE
MY SECRET DIARY
THE PRIMROSE RAILWAY CHILDREN
PROJECT FAIRY

PLENTY OF MISCHIEF
SLEEPOVERS
THE WORRY WEBSITE
BEST FRIENDS
GLUBBSLYME
THE CAT MUMMY
LIZZIE ZIPMOUTH
THE MUM-MINDER
CLIFFHANGER
BURIED ALIVE!

FOR OLDER READERS
GIRLS IN LOVE
GIRLS UNDER PRESSURE
GIRLS OUT LATE
GIRLS IN TEARS
KISS
LOVE LESSONS
LOVE, FRANKIE
BABY LOVE